BRIAN HOWELL

THE MAN WHO LOVED KURAS

AND OTHER STORIES

SALT
**MODERN
STORIES**

SALT

CROMER

PUBLISHED BY SALT PUBLISHING 2022

2 4 6 8 10 9 7 5 3 1

Copyright © Brian Howell 2022

First published in Great Britain in 2022 by
Salt Publishing Ltd
12 Norwich Road, Cromer, Norfolk NR27 0AX United Kingdom

www.saltpublishing.com

Salt Publishing Limited Reg. No. 5293401

A CIP catalogue record for this book is available from the British Library

ISBN 978 1 78463 261 8 (Paperback edition)
ISBN 978 1 78463 262 5 (Electronic edition)

Typeset in Granjon by Salt Publishing

Printed and bound in Great Britain by Clays Ltd, Elcograf S.p.A.

In memory of Sophie Wright, a beautiful friend

Contents

The Man Who Loved Kuras

As Ishii started out on one of his daily walks past the local daycare centre, the screams of the children sounded out. The centre was set beside a small wood with a modest shrine; it was in this part that the children ran around, like maniacs, like all children of their age. He had heard such cries for years, and the first thought that came to mind was almost always that a child was in danger, swiftly followed by the welcome realisation that it was quite the opposite case: they were simply expressions of natural childhood exuberance. Nested within this realisation was yet another: his own children had in all likelihood taken part in these banshee-like choruses, when they used to play there, when he and Kozue had needed to work. On those occasions, he would sometimes run out to check nothing was amiss. He could not swear on his life that he had ever witnessed them contribute to the shouting, but it was not an unreasonable assumption. Seeing him wheezing in the hallway after his return, Kozue would just laugh at his naïveté, pretty much as she did any time he was in distress.

Right now, their two children were grown and had

flown the coop, and the new generation outside played on oblivious to him and his cares, but his mind was soon on other things, in any case.

Never an eager stroller, he had grown used to these rambles since people had once more been free to go out, after several years now, anxious to make up for exercise otherwise lost in their daily working lives, now that so many worked from home and were unlikely ever to go back to working in an office. And he felt he had a purpose, too. An additional upside was that he was noticing nature and buildings, in short, everything, much more than had previously been the case.

At this time of year, late autumn, he was always fascinated by how the branches of many of the trees on his walk into town were decorated with strands of spiders' webs; annexed by the serendipity of another species' wanderings, the boughs seemed to be holding hands in a chain, almost like kids at a party, or people on stage at the end of a theatrical performance. Some of the strands were completely broken and were hoisting a lone dogwood tree's leaf mid-air as if performing some magical trick for the passers-by. Other strands seemed to be part of a complex experiment in trigonometry, the blueprint of an as-yet unachieved architecture.

It would be untrue to say that one particular part of his walk was the highlight, but a small residential area that had popped up a few years earlier had become an intriguing, if brief, accompaniment to his thoughts, and because of its proximity to his home, conveniently bookended his trips.

Having left his immediate, rather nondescript village, he would go across a main road and proceed directly into a street whose topography departed dramatically from its surroundings. It was neither one of the wealthier, traditionally walled areas with their classic *kura* storehouses, nor did it reflect the featureless modern style of building which for him had no place in any world that was deserving of a soul. A cynic would say that this street, this small community, had been designed by a modern, faceless marketing campaign team, yet, for all that, it comprised elements which seemed in search of a meaning, albeit, from where he stood, it harboured a most puzzling ambition.

Its first corner, like a chicane in motor sport, presented itself as an open invitation. There was nothing forbidding about it. Yet, within the space of a quick turn to the left and then one to the right, he felt enclosed, in a welcoming way. But it was here that the puzzle began. He could not make sense of the planning. No matter how many times he walked up and down the street, he could see no regularity to the design or architecture. True, all of the houses were roughly similar and were to all intents and purposes seemingly made for young families who had one car and probably two children. There was something hopeful about that, he thought. All good citizens, he was sure. There were attempts at uniformity, too, but it eschewed the cookie-cutter approach to so much modern town planning.

True, there were some consistencies. Almost every house, or unit, had outside it a curiously-shaped plant-holder, curious because it looked more like a pram than an addition to the garden's plant culture. Additionally, every house had a small garden light nestled in the grass, attended by some figure, a gnome or some other Disney figure, ready to illuminate the façade of its master's dominion. Needless to say, each house was constructed from the same material. But the disposition of windows, of different sizes, which for him gave a house much of its character, was in no way regular. Looking from one façade to another across the narrow street, which effectively comprised a play area for kids, whom he rarely saw here, he could never find a correspondence, except in a few cases where one doorway or window found its counterpart at a diagonal angle. But these instances were not consistent, and there was none where you might expect a direct mirroring of a structure, as you might in many suburban streets. He could not say why it occupied his mind so much, but each time he went down this street, he felt that something would one day snap into place to allow him to make sense of this location. In all the times he had passed by here, curiously, he had never spoken to anyone from any of these houses, and rarely, if ever, made eye contact, now he thought about it.

He continued on past an allotment, then down a slope by the railway line which crossed the small river and passed under the bridge. As he came out of the short underpass, he noticed the messy agglomeration of mechanical diggers and other machinery still doing work along the riverbank. He knew that further on, to his right, they had cleared much of the wilder overgrown parts along the river bank, to do God knows what. The only progress they had made to date was to add a concrete platform to the side of the river that had an intricate pattern of lozenge shapes. Perhaps it was part of some structure to strengthen the banks against flooding. Perhaps. But at this point, the intentions of the project were still unclear. And he worried that the project had probably dislodged any number of wildlife species that had happily built their homes in the sides of the river.

From the corner of his eye, as he left all that behind and turned into the main road that crossed the river, he thought he saw a piece of blue clothing in amongst the mess of machinery and building equipment he had just walked past, maybe a discarded raincoat, maybe part of some tarpaulin. He could not say for sure.

Recently, in stark contrast to his fascination with those modern buildings, perhaps as a result of his bicycle rides in the countryside, he had developed an interest in a particular type of building he had barely noticed before: the *kura*. A kura was a brick storehouse for valuable items; in previous generations it would have housed expensive kimonos as a way of protecting them from fire or earthquakes. Unlike most buildings in Japan, they were made of stone or bricks, in one case he had heard of, from compressed volcanic ash. These kuras came in many variations and sizes, though he tended to find those with a white, stuccoed exterior more appealing. He was always on the look-out for one of these. Often as not, they were partly hidden by walls around small, landed estates. Such houses were dotted all around most villages and small towns, completely subsumed by their surroundings. Given that most modern buildings were horrible eyesores, it seemed amazing to him that they did not stand out more, but, by his own admission, he was, most days, blissfully unaware of these wealthier estates. In truth, his recent fascination had stemmed from a former student, who had received a commission to work on a book illustrating kuras and happened to ask him if he knew anything about their history, Ishii's own subject being art history. The link was tenuous, but he had covered many aspects of world art and architecture in his courses. He had told the student he didn't know much at all about these particular buildings, but he would be willing to do a little research for him, as the student had piqued his interest, and certainly Ishii had plenty of time nowadays.

In truth, gaining admittance to one of these kuras had by no means been easy. Given their history of being used to store valuable items, he suspected that owners would necessarily be reluctant to allow just any old stranger in to poke around. However, he had had a stroke of luck recently and through a friend of a friend was in fact on his way to view his very first.

His walk to the kura took him further along his regular walk, past a rice paddy, from which the recording of a peregrine falcon designed to scare off crows now sounded, along a busy street, then down a shaded path adjacent to a park where couples usually ambled with their children on their days off. He had done the same twenty-five years earlier with Kozue and their own children. That was a time when he had less sophisticated hobbies than now, when he was content to hunch over a book or watch television and keep an eye on Tatsuya and Riko as they grew up, content in the knowledge that Kozue had everything in check and that he only needed to be present as a father figure. Now, computers and all their attendant devices took up – and wasted – much more of his time, albeit the Internet offered him a kind of relaxation he could not obtain from other things.

The past blurring into a familiar haze, he now made a right across a small canal onto a busy road that ran along a football stadium, mercifully empty today, and approached the local shrine, a grand, significant edifice that he had always been in danger of taking for granted. Today was a weekday, so there were few families around, he was relieved to find. Skirting the shrine, he was soon at the meeting point.

He was met by a man of about forty, which surprised him a little, along with his even younger wife, who had her daughter in train. The girl, in pigtails, was perhaps six or seven, and got up in a frilly velvet red one-piece with white trim. She seemed extremely excited. He smiled at her as best he could, which she met with a look of puzzlement and then a kind of shyness, which she tried to mask by looking up into the sky. The couple themselves seemed unusually friendly and almost in a hurry for him to see the property. He had really been lucky to find such an accommodating couple, he congratulated himself.

Exchanging the customary gifts, they took him down a few streets back in the direction from which he had come, for a while.

The kura itself was disappointingly small and not the white-walled kind he had been expecting, but this was more than made up for by the beautiful Oya stone from a famous quarry, as he learned.

'It's no more than a store cupboard, really,' the man explained. 'We inherited it from my father, you know.'

His wife smiled as if obedient to some pre-planned set of manners. He thought it no more than the typical deference of a woman to her husband in these parts. Yet, she was atypical for a mother, in some ways, with her blonde-dyed hair, and he thought he had seen her put out a cigarette in the street as he approached them.

'So,' the man said, 'would you like to look inside?'

'Oh definitely, if that's O.K.'

'Absolutely.'

The man pulled hard on the red iron door, which had on it a tastefully designed plaque displaying the family name. Hesitantly, as if visiting a relative for the first time in years, he edged in. He felt the man's hand on his shoulder, as if pushing him slightly in his eagerness for the older man to see the interior. But Ishii was so consumed by his need to see what the interior was like that he soon forgot about it.

Inside, there were basic wooden shelves with boxes of different sizes full of junk, but he wasn't interested in what the couple were storing, as he had told them; he just wanted to get a feel for the interior structure. The wood itself was disappointingly new, to his mind. About twenty years old, as was told.

'You can go up, but we can't open the windows.'

'Sure,' he agreed. He could, however, study their iron-work grill design, which reminded him of the exterior door. Something about it made him think of art nouveau. On the underside of the pitched roof he could see patches of what looked like concrete smeared somewhat amateurishly as some kind of reinforcement to the traditional material.

There wasn't much more to see, but he was grateful for being allowed to investigate this much. By now, back outside, the girl was on her father's shoulders and swaying in a way that made him nervous, as it had always done with Rika. As the father came closer to him, the man reached up without warning as if to brush off something from the back of his visitor's head. As he did so, the girl made a sudden movement and seemed to be toppling over. Ishii grabbed her by the waist to break her fall, but she ended up somehow in his arms, wrapped around him, laughing in his face. He just managed to stay on his feet.

The mother didn't seem flustered, but the man was profusive in his thanks.

'Oh, thank you so much. She's always doing that! It was a spider, by the way. Somehow got in your hair.'

The girl, in her almost Victorian dress, was dancing around in the street now, the incident already extinguished in her mind, it seemed. Why dress such a tomboy in clothes like that? he mused.

'Well, I'm glad she's O.K. I'm so grateful for your time. It's been a treat! I'd better let you three go.'

'Our pleasure, totally. Any time.'

Some weeks later, he heard from Kozue of the disappearance of a young girl from their locality a week or so earlier. In addition to the fugitive nature of so many human interactions nowadays, he *had* noticed an even more circumspect attitude to people's comings and goings lately, he reflected. Maybe this news explained it. It was less pronounced, he noticed, as he got further into town.

'Be careful; people are very suspicious nowadays,' Kozue said as he went out on one of his walks.

'Because of the girl? I hardly think they would be suspicious of a retired prof like me.'

'Hmm. I sometimes wonder what you get up to on your walks,' she said in a way that was not totally typical and made him wonder how serious she was. Would she stand by him if he were ever accused of any crime, no matter what? Wasn't that part of any partner's duty? Of course, it wouldn't be expected if the spouse *were* actually guilty. If *he* were guilty. That would be asking too much. On the other hand, he thought, anyone can accuse you of anything any time, if they don't like you. Especially nowadays.

He turned his thoughts to cheerier things. Today, he would be trying his luck with another kura, hoping to be allowed in to see a larger one this time. It was hard enough to actually catch anyone at home, at least as far as the owners went. Now it might be even harder, with all these funny looks going around. But you never knew.

He took a circuitous route into town, to see if he could persuade the owner of one of those classic white-faced kuras to let him in. He had passed this one many times, not thinking about where the entrance was, until he had stumbled upon it coming from a totally different direction a few days before. On this occasion, he was in luck. A woman in her sixties came out to greet him. Dressed in wellingtons and wearing a fishing hat that almost all older people wore in these parts, she seemed to be trying to suppress a look of sly amusement as she took his business card from his old university post, but she had her wits about her as she sized him up, seeming to like what she saw, and said he could look inside only, as it was too dangerous to walk on the boards as they were rotted. Bizarrely, she demonstrated this by walking in herself, by which time he already saw himself facing a lawsuit for having her endanger herself. Mercifully, she came out unscathed, so he wasn't sure what exactly the purpose of such a display had been. Nevertheless, he got a good look inside and outside, in a way he couldn't have done from taking photos over the wall that gave onto the nearby road.

Emboldened by his good fortune, he set off for his walk into town. He was soon once again walking down the street that boasted the new houses, in effect a small, ungated community that filled him with a sense of longing every time he passed by it.

On this occasion, as he walked into the street, for no reason that he particularly understood, he waved at a man overseeing his two children, a boy and a girl. The man looked at him blankly. Ishii felt horrible. *What on Earth are you doing?* he scolded himself. *Are you crazy?*

Then, having turned the corner, he spotted something he dreaded: a police car, with two police officers talking to someone. It was right at the end of the street, and he considered turning back, but that would look very bad. He *always* worried he would be stopped by the police, even though they would have no reason to stop him. And in this region, the police were by repute bumbling and bored, if not docile. In all likelihood, the highlight of their day was stopping schoolkids for wearing earphones on their bikes, while drivers of articulated lorries drove with impunity with one hand on the wheel and their other on their mobile phones, and motorcyclists had music and who knows what else piped into their helmets. Having said that, he did know that the conviction rate of people brought to court was in the ninety-nine percentile.

He walked on, expecting to see more children playing, given it was a Sunday, but the street was empty. He went past the police officers somewhat self-consciously, extracting himself gingerly from their presence with a near-audible sigh of relief.

It was only as he approached town again that he had the

idea of revisiting the couple's small kura. He would take some more photos of the exterior, as he was unsatisfied with the ones he had taken on the day. He hoped he didn't draw attention, but why should he? It was a few steps away from a quite famous shrine.

Satisfied with what he had achieved this day, he did his shopping in town and went back home with a skip in his step, but by the main roads, not the usual way this time.

In the following weeks, unbeknownst to Ishii, while he had continued to badger strangers with his requests for access to their kuras, a steady trickle of complaints had started to make its way to local police boxes and stations about an avuncular gentleman purporting to be a former professor doing research into one particular type of building. Not even Kozue knew anything of this, but she was becoming visibly vexed by the number of calls she had had to answer from the handful of people actually willing to let her husband see their storehouses: they entailed a number of call-backs, especially because he often was not at home when they called and he didn't possess a mobile phone. To her credit, but also to his annoyance, Kozue was not the retiring type of person who raised her voice to a shrill level of politeness on the phone as many women were still expected to do, so she may have put a few people's backs up when she took a message. At the same time, during this period, news had filtered down that the missing girl had been found, dead, but it was not being reported where and if the death was suspicious.

On his return from another one of his trips one day,

Kozue met him with the dreadful news that the police had called and wanted to interview him. *Him.*

'The police! Whatever for?' he shot out.

To him, it seemed she took this the wrong way, as an accusation that she was in some way responsible for such a development. This was her way, though he realised that on this occasion he really should not have reacted as he did. He needed her on his side.

'They didn't come in and look around, did they?'

'No, of course not. How could they?'

'If you let them . . .'

'Ah, if I let them! Do you think I'm crazy?'

'I'm sorry. Calm down,' he said, adding a belated 'Please'.

'But . . . there's nothing here that . . . would get you into trouble?'

'I don't know how you can ask that,' he said. 'But then who knows, these days?'

'Now you're worrying me!'

He smiled, saying, 'I'm just joking. You don't have to worry.'

'Anyway, they said you had to go to the station, as soon as you can.'

'I suppose that is reasonable. Give me the phone number, then.'

He rang the detective who was in charge and arranged to go to the station that evening, but he couldn't help commenting to Kozue after the call.

'I just can't imagine what it could be about. I just can't imagine.'

Setting out as it was beginning to become dark, Ishii racked his brains about this development. There was nothing he could prepare in his mind to say to the *police*. He had never had any but the most innocent contact with them his whole life. He could only think of trivial things, such as asking for directions. He had never committed a crime, been accused of one, been in a fight. Nothing. The only crime he could be accused of was a thought crime! But then surely almost everyone could, if that was the criterion.

Admittedly, he lived in a world of fantasy, especially nowadays. He was certainly prepared to admit that much. Actually, he *was* capable of imagining anything. When people say they can't imagine such-and-such, they are liars. *There is nothing you can't imagine.* He had said that often enough to friends, when the occasion arose. The sentence just needs to be uttered and there you have it! You imagined it. No matter how horrible the action – for it was usually an action.

So maybe, just maybe, Ishii knew now why he would never attend his interview. Instead, he would visit the couple's kura. He would lurk in the area for a while, till the tourists dwindled away. There was no point going home. He knew the DNA was on him, to start with. Somewhere on him, surely. It was spread around his home, too. He was so forgetful that he couldn't even remember what it was he was wearing at the time, or even if Kozue had cleaned his clothes since. This way, he would at least have an excuse. If it were still there, in his home, which it couldn't be. *Could* it?

He would force open the iron door and make his way upstairs. He did not expect to find anything but the memories, but he knew they would find *him*, curled in a ball. Then he thought of the curious dress. Maybe that was still there. That he would like. Maybe there were some other trophies. His last thoughts were of her young, tinkling voice and the touch of her skin like a feathered leaf as he remembered her falling . . . into his arms. His angel.

Dead Centre

Dear Dara, Prague, 9th August, 1999

I feel very strange this morning because I woke up with an unusual longing. I was dreaming that I was a calf whale beached on the shore of some exotic land. Not very far away was my mother. The men were cutting into her and the blood was running into the foamy water. She was crying, and I felt an overwhelming sensation of regret that I had not always wanted to trail behind her. I started to cry too, and the men came to me.

Then I woke up and realised it was an item on the World Service coming from my clock radio. It was about whale cullers in Japan, I believe. Why do people do such things?

It's strange that I should write this letter to you today because it was on this day in 1969 that they discovered the terrible things that happened to Roman Polanski's wife in Beverley Hills. It was also on this day in 1917 that Kafka (about whom I plan to do some research here) had his famous haemorrhage, which, far from being the end of the road for him, gave him inspiration. You see, not all violent events are nasty. Think of birth, for example. Anyway, I only mention it because I have a thing about dates and coincidences. And I hope you don't think I have too morbid an imagination.

I really am sorry I didn't tell you I was going off like this, but I just didn't have the courage. Besides, I saw something where you work that sent shivers down my back, but I didn't feel like mentioning it at the time. I still don't know if you are aware of what disturbed me so much. It all makes little difference now. And in fact I had decided not to contact you ever again, but then memories of you started to follow me around like a shoal of fish, darting one moment this way, another moment that, making me quite dizzy.

I sat down on a bench somewhere and started to catch these fish in my mind. Then, like parts of an old photo of a loved one that has torn in four or five different places (the sort you often make copies of in the lab), I put these together, your long blonde hair, the occasional freckle under your grey-blue eyes, your uncommon figure that does not constrict, but rather flows on as part of you. It makes me think of my efforts to find the centre of that picture of Irena on the Charles Bridge standing against the Vltava. This image started to pull on me as if it were the missing melody of a song of which I could until then only make out the lyrics. I began to imagine her as you. But, of course, it is her picture on your wall there, isn't it?

Do you remember how we first met? My next stop is Paris, a fitting place to write a love letter from, I think.

Love,
Alex

Dead Centre

It was an original way of drawing attention, I have to say that much. I wouldn't have given you a second glance, otherwise, I feel sure. How could I forget? I think this photo says it all, don't you think?

I was standing outside the Safeway arcade at Wood Green. To the right you can see the photo lab, to the left the Safeway teashop with a surprising assortment of customers – what do they find so irresistible about the prospect of sipping tea to this dreary parade of truculent shoppers? Whatever it is, it's always pretty full. I am trying to banish such thoughts as I smile meekly for you to finish off the roll of film. If you look closely, you'll see yourself reflected in one of the glass doors to my right. I would never, going by the rest of your efforts on the same roll, have guessed you capable of such amateurishness. Maybe you were just over-excited by my compliance?

The first time your photos came through, the colour balance had gone, so I had to put them through again. Then I was struck by the photos themselves, the sometimes weirdly out-of-kelter shots of doorways and arches, as if you had stumbled on a place you had only previously seen in a nightmare, that had haunted you your whole life and you were now trying to make it concrete, come to terms with it. You seemed to have achieved this by taking alternate views of the same places in completely rigid, balanced compositions. I swear that I could have measured the distances from each edge to the centre and they would have been the same down to the last fraction of a millimetre. I couldn't help thinking of that when we made love. With anyone else I would have laughed.

Whether conscious of it or not, I couldn't resist quickly sorting through the photos when you came in to collect them.

'It's Prague, isn't it?' I had said, not expecting to be disabused.

'Yes, I was there last summer . . . Haven't you already checked through them?'

I wasn't sure if you were implying some criticism of our working methods, but I tried not to sound offended.

'Of course, we always check through them when they first come off. I was just curious,' I explained.

I separated the photo you had taken of me outside the shop from the others. You seemed momentarily anxious.

'Could I keep it?' you said expectantly.

'Why?' I said, perhaps a little too provocatively.

'It's such a well-balanced picture,' you said without a trace of embarrassment.

'Do you mind my asking what you do?'

'I'm . . . getting a portfolio together . . . to get into college.'

'Oh,' I said. I couldn't think of a way of prolonging the conversation, so I sealed the photos, including the one of me, in an envelope and gave them to you.

After that, I noticed how you would quickly launch yourself into the arcade on the way to Safeways, not looking in, but somehow self-conscious, like an animal constantly aware of movement around it, aware that perhaps I was looking out for you. Eventually, one evening, when no one else was in the shop, you mustered the courage to ask me out for a drink.

◊

'Your arms.'

 'What?'

 'They have to be the same distance apart.'

 'I suppose you want them tied up as well?' I said, trying to mask my fear with a tone of self-assured but tempered offence.

 Perhaps it was not quite what I had expected, because you went limp very quickly.

 'No, it's not like that. It's just the first time. I promise.'

 A likely story, I thought, but you were so gentle, pushing at my skin as if testing thin ice. I thought of your photos of Prague, the Vltava running under the Charles Bridge like a gigantic eel, your efforts to find the centre of the picture, which in this case had failed. You had been too aware of it moving. Rivers were difficult, you had said.

 You pushed my arms out as if you were stretching a canvas ready to be primed, oiling every part of me with your saliva. Our sweat merged to leave an aggregate of temporary impressions.

 You had been a dolphin, or a shark, but now that intensity, the same that had been in your pictures, was gone, and you were like a male version of Magritte's stranded half-fish/half-woman, slumped on top of me. In my mind's eye, I searched for clues in the photos – memorised now from the distorted set I had printed first time – something to give you more substance, but it was gone.

 Then you disappeared. I would perhaps not have

thought of you again, except as a beautiful memory, had not Ros noticed that little clue I had missed.

The photos of Prague were hastily fanned out like playing cards on the marble-top table. Ros wore a quizzical expression.

'So what's all the fuss?' she said, unimpressed. 'Don't you think he's talented?' I almost pleaded.'

She quickly scanned them again, though I sensed her heart wasn't in it. Then she stopped at a photo of the girl standing in a rather uncomfortable pose in the middle of the thoroughfare where people walked up and down the Charles Bridge. She was perhaps embarrassed that so much attention was being directed at her. The picture was characteristically taken in the dead centre of the pathway. Alex had quickly dismissed it for not being 'balanced' enough. She had kept fidgeting, he had said. But it wasn't this aspect that was worrying Ros.

'You didn't say you met him there,' she said, turning a suggestive smile on me.

'What d'you mean? Of course I didn't.'

'And he didn't say he saw you there?'

'No. What are you getting at?'

'Look here,' she said, pointing to a group of anonymous tourists slightly to the left of the girl.

Her finger rested on a loose red T-shirt worn by a brunette wearing dark glasses. It was slightly out of focus, far from suggesting her inclusion was intentional. I had noticed it before. Then it dawned on me what Ros was thinking.

'It's you, isn't it?' she said, almost accusingly.

'Well, I did walk across the bridge a few times, but it could be someone else.'

'Come on, it's you. You could get it blown up if you're still not sure.'

I kept looking at it, trying to convince myself it wasn't me, or if it was, that it was just coincidence, but too many other thoughts were assailing me.

Ros drew back, taking my silence for some kind of admission. I made one last attempt to reason it away.

'But I was there in June, and he's only just brought these in. In September.'

'It looks like you're lucky he's not around anymore . . .'

'That's the problem,' I said. 'I actually miss him.'

◊

Dear Dara   27th August, 1990

Guess where this is coming from? Yes, the Pont Neuf. Makes me think of the Beatles – Number Nine, Number Nine, Number Nine . . . And of course, I wrote to you on the . . . th (fill in as necessary.) And 9 is a multiple of . . . which is how many . . . as well as being a divisor of . . . But I should not divagate like this. (I said I had a thing about numbers.)

When will we . . . meet again? Sorry, I couldn't resist that one.

I have an image of you walking around these places, shadowing me unknowingly. You look lost. I come up to you outside a museum and you start. Your camera drops to the ground, smashing the lens. I hold it up, examining your striated image in the glass, like beautiful lacerations. I offer to replace it. We sit down, have a coffee. I don't have the money with me. But you give me your address, your London one. I don't have the courage to ask where you are staying in Paris. We chat about art, you love the Impressionists, I the old masters. But we find a meeting point somewhere, a point of convergence.

But this is unfair. I am not alone. Of course, it was on this bridge that I photographed Erika, and I presume you have sussed that one out too by now. I would ask you to come here with me, but I feel you will draw the inevitable conclusion from this photo.

Write to me, in your secret diary; type the words into my genes, digitally. There will be no intermediate stage. No one need ever know.

Love,
Alex

Dara's Diary   1st September, 1990

I tried again to put you out of my mind. I only succeeded for a while, but it wasn't totally my fault.

I had gone to Paris and stayed with an old friend. He was the only lover I'd had since you, and even then it was more for old times' sake. A bit half-hearted, really. I spent most of my time taking photos of buildings in preparation for my architecture course, but each time – which was often – I was confronted with symmetry, I inevitably thought of you.

Then I developed someone's photos of Paris, one of

which – this time there was no mistaking it – included me, though still not exactly at the centre of the picture. It was in front of the overpowering art deco of the Musée d'Orsay, next to the elephant sculpture. I was myself trying to take my own picture of the canopy over the entrance after giving up trying to get the whole building in in one shot because of the lack of space. What was driving you to keep your distance like this?

Dear Dara   Amsterdam, 31st August, 1990

I know that you have probably already replied to my last epistle, but I have very little chance of ever reading it, as I have a busy itinerary, as you can see. It sometimes occurs to me that the history of human relations is just like this, a sequence of letters being written to people who never receive the ones intended for them but go on writing their replies, which are in turn never received. But I know your diary entries, your imaginary letters, in intimate detail, even before they flow through the forking paths of your dreams to the tips of your gentle fingers.

It reminds me of the apocryphal story of the executioner who could never shoot his victim until he had gazed into his face and relived his victim's life from childhood on. After this procedure, he never hesitated to carry out his duty; he was always convinced that his victim's life could never have followed any path except the one to which life's rich delta had now brought him. Except with the last face that confronted him: his own. Well, now I am facing what I have imagined and feared for years.

I'm standing on the little bridge in front of the

Rijksmuseum, just down from Hobbemakade. It's quite fitting, because I can see my life stretching out in front of me like Hobbema's avenue of trees in our own National Gallery in England. But when I go inside, I imagine you reading this letter like Vermeer's *Lady in Blue*.

I shan't say write soon, because it's unlikely that your letters would reach their destination. Perhaps you should put them in a drawer somewhere in a neat pile for me to savour one day?

Love,
Alex

◊

When I told Ros, her reaction was immediate and decisive. 'Well you have to go to Amsterdam,' she said as she wiped between her legs, threw the paper into the lavatory bowl, and flushed. I never asked her why she never bothered to close the door.

'You think it's some kind of code?'

'Uh-huh.'

'If only I knew for sure.'

I thought of his lithe limbs, the martellato of his hands on my arms and buttocks, the glissando of his tongue tip on my nipples.

'You're right. I have to go.'

'You know where he'll be waiting.'

I was intrigued by the strange church-like structure of the Rijksmuseum, both inside and out. I visited the place every day for a week, gradually familiarising myself with that country's past through its achingly sharp cameos of everyday life, which gave the impression that nothing else existed outside these renditions of a near-perfect world. They seemed unperturbed by any past and even less by a future.

What could he see in that blue lady whose very mystery was aided by the radial craquelure of the paint? I stood in front of that many times, too, imagining the content of her letter, reading it over to the rhythm of the water in a ubiquitous canal, inventing dialogues that unrolled outside the frame, seeing the birth of the lady's child.

It was my last day in the town. I came out of the museum to take one more look at the building from the bridge. It was nearly dark as I leaned on the railing and gazed.

The sound I heard then could be described as the whirring rattle of some reptile's movement, perhaps the exaggerated opening or closing of a huge eye, or a tail swishing momentarily.

Or the long exposure of an aperture eager to wrest from the near-dark the last filaments of light, the abrupt guillotine-like ending as sharp and final as a car crash.

What I saw had all of these, because, taken by you, it enclosed everything, as if, in being espied by that clicking eye, the very maculae that made up my form were competing with the light rushing into that hole like birds being sucked into the jet engines of a plane, oblivious. I felt like a character in a film irised into a single, tiny point, constricted into blackness.

This is what you want now, isn't it?

A figure, a brunette, leaning in the near-dark against the railing of a bridge which looks over to a famous museum is seen as a snapshot. Darkness, surprised by its own alacrity, shrouds and encumbers her, embraces her like Klimt's cloaked harbingers of death.

◊

She plunges, into darkness, to emerge into the watery, blood-red, chemical existence which affords her a new birth. Now your features are clearer. Your steady gaze comes into view as you deliver me from this murky, liquid bed. You embrace me, breathe on me, your breath is warm.

I look out on a strange, unseen environment now, seeing a gallery of semi-ecstatic visages. Opposite, a mirror. I see myself, the centrepiece, yes, just as you wanted it. Irena, Erika, and me.

The Mask

'There's no art to find the mind's construction in the face.'

Macbeth

THERE HAD BEEN no other experience like it for Yuki. Perhaps it was a kind of drug, an addiction, but a subtle one, to be sure.

It started with a simple recommendation to try out a new dentist. He had been grinding his teeth for some time and had felt that his regular dentist no longer cared about his welfare. This dentist wasn't even interested in making money out of Yuki, it seemed. He was just indifferent. Where his regular dentist had been local, the new one was located in Tokyo, in an area between Ueno and Akihabara, also known as Electric Town. He had been to these places before, of course, but seldom to the area in between.

His new dentist, a man in his mid-fifties, was polite and friendly and wrote him a letter to take to a university hospital, but Yuki never went. In a sense, he lost his way. He could not describe it in any other manner. He became distracted by what turned out to be an endless round of teeth polishing and cleanings which started with him, a man of forty, being shown how to brush his teeth. Not once, but on several occasions. However, this series of tutorials was not administered by the dentist who ran the clinic, but rather by a female hygienist with a nice manner; as far as he could see, she was attractive.

'As far as he could see' was to be taken literally: he simply never saw her face as she was always wearing a mask. But that was OK. He could see her eyes and ninety-five per cent of her body, and the main thing was that she was doing a very good job.

What he remembered from that first cleaning session, then, was not so much his attraction to her as the fact that he accepted so calmly the idea of being pampered and the accompanying enticement of buying their range of inexpensive accessories, which included their simple, cheap toothbrushes (one a month) and their interdental brushes (a pack of four per month). The latter were a novelty for him and by far and away more tactile, invasive, and pleasurable than he could have imagined, as he stood in front of the mirror at home in the evening and in the morning inserting them into the gaps in his front and back teeth. He was wary of overusing them and forcing them where they surely could not go, though when he asked about overuse on his return he was gently disabused.

On his second visit he began to notice the local area more, the antiquarian shops, the secondhand junk shops, the lively market on the edges of Ueno, the ramen shops of the kind you found anywhere in the country, steak houses, 'family' restaurants, and in fact the innumerable restaurants, generally. He began to wonder why so many businesses were concentrated around what was after all a very mundane overground train station. The more famous Akihabara and Ueno had a greater reason for existing, to his mind, and yet this place had been here just as long, probably, waiting for him. He knew it was an irrational feeling, but it was real.

And alongside the usual shops and specialists such as a whole shop devoted to the paraphernalia of the idiotic sport of golf, he started to notice the occasional doorway or sign, usually advertising massage.

It became clear as early as his second, maybe his third, visit to the dentist's, however, that something else would keep him coming to the area for some time: the matter of cleaning the 'pockets' around his teeth. They called it deep pocket cleaning, and the expression had an appeal for him he could not quite explain. This was despite the fact that however many X-rays they showed him, he felt he would not ever quite understand what or where these pockets resided, exactly. He knew only that they were back there somewhere, minute, but significant enough to let his imagination picture small grooves that were being chipped away at to remove the tartar that was accumulating there and endangering the stability of his teeth. Occasionally, his mind conjured a castle whose walls were slowly being undermined by soldiers working away at its foundations underground.

So on that second visit he became aware as one becomes aware of something that one has taken for granted for a length of time, that the hygienist, Mariko, was still wearing her mask. He was not even afforded the opportunity of seeing her face for even the brief few minutes when dentists and their assistants sometimes lowered their masks when they were not doing close work or when they appeared in the reception area. Consequently, he felt licensed to observe her eyes more attentively than might otherwise have been the case. Pleasingly, her eyes were the type that he preferred and many of his countrymen and women felt embarrassed by: single-lidded, with a pronounced epicanthic fold. He had lost count of the number of past girlfriends who had pouted with displeasure at such an unlucky throw of the evolutionary die, usually when he had complimented them.

Naturally, he wondered if he would ever get the chance to do exactly that with Mariko. It was a long hill to climb, though, to go from being ministered to impersonally to going on a date, which would almost definitely result in his having to switch clinics afterwards. He had to put it from his mind, and for the time being that was fairly easy, given his propensity to drift off in the chair, a guilty pleasure, though he did not know why.

'I'm just going to lower your chair now,' she said, not for the first time. He never really tired of these accommodating punctuations to a procedure he would soon become very used to. In fact, he found it rather winning of her.

Then, 'I'm just going to do a little mouth irrigation now.'

And so it would go. If it was a simple cleaning, he would feel that chiselling sensation to remove the tartar around and between his teeth, a sensation which he actually found pleasant, unless a nerve was touched. He would have been the first, however, to make it clear that he was no masochist.

And he felt genuinely discomfited not being able to swallow with ease, but there was a sense of comfort in being entirely at the mercy of another person under such a regime, to be sure, not least when the hygienist's small chest occasionally pressed up against the back of his head when she had to stand behind him.

Most sessions proceeded in this way, with him making only the barest small talk with Mariko. Part of him resented the number of trips he would have to make to see this deep pocket cleaning through, yet another part was happy to see the process extended like this, for both the opportunity to see Mariko and to be lightly pinioned by the triangle made by her slim arms and hands.

Added to all this, he was becoming more curious about the area around the station. A few times, as he walked from the station, he had seen the same young man, who had shoulderlength brown hair and a permanently startled look, standing by one of the exits in the lee of the raised train platform. Perhaps he had seen the same young women, too, hurrying determinedly into buildings where they worked.

On perhaps his fifth visit now, he wondered about the furtive businesses being run in the area. In his mind, sometimes, he saw a narrow staircase with uninviting metal doors and cryptic signs and had the sensation of both being drawn in and repelled. Perhaps he would enquire nevertheless.

'That's you done for today, then.' Mariko's words dug him out of his reverie.

When he exited the surgery, it was already dark and raining, but he did not feel like going home. There was something missing, something he hadn't thought of that he felt to be on the edges of awareness. On the corner of the street the surgery was located in there was a handy shop that sold cheap cans of some of his favourite drinks and chocolates, so he headed there. Feeling vaguely satisfied at this little find, he started to walk to the station, but as it was a Friday evening and he hadn't lined up anything, he walked across a busy main street into the very lively market that sheltered under the raised train tracks. It was a muddle of side streets, stalls, nooks, and cross-paths that reminded him of scenes from films set in North Africa. After some while trudging around and from his knowledge of previous forays, he knew that one edge of this market was bounded by clubs and what were probably hostess bars, in which he had never had any interest. Just a big scam for salary men. Plastic bag in hand, then, he stood there on the corner of one of the streets he had just come down, and for the first time he wondered if he was doing this in the absurd hope that he might bump into Mariko by chance. He surely would if he did it often enough, of course, but the odds could just as easily be that he could walk though a wall, which he had read could happen, except that it would probably take longer than the eventual history of the universe to come about. Or it could happen with his next step.

In the meantime, he spotted what he had probably not wanted to admit to himself all along: an advertisement on the ground floor for a relaxing massage on the third floor of a nearby building. It showed a woman lying on a tropical beach, and he thought it was rather ironic for such a business to be showing the sort of client that was probably the last person to come to them for a massage.

He was drawn to the idea, but at the same time, part of him did not want anything inappropriate to take place. Inappropriate to whom? a voice inside him said.

He went up the ill-lit staircase, which was surprisingly quiet, to his mind. Not sure of himself, he knocked on a door on the second floor and a young woman in a Bo-Peep outfit came up to him. Thinking this was the same business as advertised outside, he asked for a price list, but as soon as he was given it, he realised this was a different place, out of his financial league.

He made his apologies and went on up to the top of the stairs, where a dowdily dressed middle-aged Chinese woman was speaking to a man of about his own age and looking through a brochure of photos of young women, all Chinese. When his turn came, he determined that he could not exactly know what he was going to get for his money, let alone know what the rooms were like, so he made his excuses, saying he would come back some time. He half-meant it. The woman had been friendly, and the whole experience had not been totally dispiriting. He had dipped his toe in, without taking the plunge.

On his next visit, on the train journey into town, he was touched by the sight of an attractive woman practising a dance routine. Supporting herself lightly on a vertical handrail, she seemed to be running through a very limited part of a flamenco routine. There was nothing flamboyant about what she was doing; on the contrary, she was concentrating so much that she must have been almost oblivious to the few people on the carriage who noticed her. He admired such singlemindedness. That someone could almost disappear within themself like this, almost hide in plain sight, comforted him. He would like to have asked her if it indeed was flamenco she was rehearsing, but it would have been uncool, and he did not want to disturb her.

This fortunate event almost succeeded in taking his mind off a familiar habit of his but ended up reinforcing it: counting the number of people wearing masks on the train. In contrast to the woman, their way of hiding was crass – and antisocial. Opposite him were two young, probably attractive (though you could not exactly be sure) women in their thirties chatting away quite contentedly, as if half the features of their faces weren't indecipherable. He spotted two middleaged men with masks, one sitting, one standing, as well as a teenager. He could not explain exactly what annoyed him so much about this practice, but it was something to do with the way the masks made one focus on the wearers' eyes, and especially how they made those eyes seem as if they were targeting him, in contrast to the way Mariko's eyes seemed totally welcoming.

At the surgery, he was told he would need an injection, as the deep pocket cleaning might be particularly hard on his gums this time, so, as Mariko went off to one of the many partitioned spaces, he surrendered himself to the least pleasant aspect by far of any session, barring having a tooth extracted, something which he had not experienced since childhood and was determined never to let happen again. He could still hear the dentist from long, long ago shouting at him how he was a coward. So ingrained was the memory that he could remember her thick black-framed glasses and over-sized fake gold earrings.

In this case, the injections were done by what must

have been a young trainee dentist, as Yuki felt a certain unsteadiness in the man's hand. It was not that Yuki was hurt in any way, rather that the trainee seemed to be taking extra-special care to steady himself. And it was not just one injection, but several.

In such instances, Yuki found it calming to think of his Jimi Hendrix collection, of the many different CDs he had, official and non-official, studio and live performances, not to mention the various versions he had downloaded from the Internet. Trying to remember what he had learned about the various live versions of Jimi's famous standards and how they had been messed with and corrected and updated over the years was enough to make him forget his nervousness for a while. The different masterings on CD of a handful of the posthumous compilations was a mind-bogglingly complicated area on its own. At the same time, in his head, he was listening to a favourite solo, and, strangely, he thought, if he were to experience a sharp pain from the needle and it were to coincide with one of the high notes on Jimi's guitar, it would somehow mitigate that pain, if not dissipate it. But luckily, there was no sharp pain on this occasion.

When Mariko reappeared, her face bound by her mask as usual, his bottom lip was already feeling numb. He managed to exchange a few pleasantries with her, but he was feeling a little sleepy even before she started clean-ing. He could not be sure, but he thought, before his eyes closed and his mind started wandering again, that he heard himself invite her to have a coffee with him.

He was walking along a dark, narrow corridor, being led by

a woman. The hand was soft to the touch. The décor was brownish orange, and there was a strong smell of incense. He noticed drab nylon sheets at intervals on either side, covering what were probably small cubicles. He heard a knocking against one wall and stopped to listen, but the hand pulled him on. She gave him a towel and told him to step into the shower. She insisted on him putting his phone in a waterproof bag and taking it with him into the shower, where he hung it on a hook. After checking the flow and temperature, she directed the shower head on him.

He woke with a start as he realised that he had fallen asleep in the middle of cleaning.

'So,' she said when she was finished. 'Which date is good for you?'

'Date?'

'For coffee.'

'But . . .'

I don't even know what you look like.

He could hardly say that, though.

'Oh, oh, yes, I think any day is fine,' he said, pulling himself together. *'Any* day?'

They set a date for the following week, the day after his next appointment, as it turned out. It was a busy surgery, and she had only the one day off.

'I'll meet you downstairs' were her last words and, as she said them, she pulled down on her mask, almost dramatically, as if she were demonstrating a mundane but necessary procedure, revealing thin lips, a small jaw, and very slightly prominent teeth, before, just as suddenly, letting it snap back into place. He decided in the end that she had performed the action absent-mindedly, as someone does at home when no one else is around.

The woman was about thirty, her hair reaching down to her shoulder blades; her breasts were soft and puffy, yielding to pressure like small, slightly deflated balloons, a sensation he adored. She showed him a picture of a village in China on her iPhone. He felt it could have been on another planet, it looked so unfamiliar.

With a start, he suddenly wondered where his own phone was. If they got hold of that, who knows what they could do with his data. But then he remembered that they had insisted on him putting it in a waterproof bag and taking it with him into the shower.

She pushed him gently onto the narrow futon so that he lay flat on his back. Before he had expected it, her head was already at his crotch, working on him. Whilst he took pleasure from what was happening, he found his mind wandering. He liked her cleanliness, the strangely dry texture of her hair, and what was almost a non-smell on her. He feared the raw smell of women more than anything. Almost any bad smell could put him off a partner whilst in the act. But perhaps it was all blanketed by the intensity of the incense in the place.

He thought of the picture on her mobile phone. Why did she make such a connection with him? Why did she even want to make such a connection? He stroked her back, moving his hand down that shallow defile to her buttocks.

She hadn't looked up at him since she had started. That was good, he thought, though it would be nice to remember her face.

Still, he found himself thinking now of her village, particularly of whether she had a child. He could just imagine that she had a mother looking after her young son or daughter right now, while she did this to him. Then, he started asking himself where the money was going, how much she kept of it in the end. There must be a trail. How much of it trickled back to her family in the village in China? How long would she have to go on doing this?

As he stood in the alcove adjusting his umbrella, about to step out into the dark and the warm rain, a figure blocked him. It was the man with shoulder-length, slightly scary hair and drab clothes. They made eye contact. Did this man guess or know something about him? More pertinently, was he judging Yuki? Maybe he even worked there in some capacity, because he went up the stairs in the direction Yuki had come from.

He realised he was back in the market; he had hardly registered it before going up to the place, having walked around so long. He didn't like the look of some of the vendors, many of whom appeared foreign, quite a few being Chinese. The market wasn't really crowded enough for him to need to push against anyone, but he felt as if he were pushing into soft currents of flesh and clammy air. Then he realised he was a little dizzy, and stumbled. Something told him he had to get off the street into the station or he would drown in people, faces, objects.

On the way home he realised he wanted to go back to the woman even if it meant before his date with Mariko, as hypocritical as that made him feel. He found himself trying in his mind to reconstruct her features, her bony, angular cheeks, her thin arms, and doll-like frame, a frame that could be adjusted almost like that of a marionette. By contrast, the masseuse was fuller-bodied, more womanly, in a sense. And then he thought of all of the things he could have done with her in the room which he had not dared although he had licence to do so, for a price. He wished he had a photo of Mariko, or at least some contact on social media but he didn't even have her email address yet!

On that first date, his heart dipped a little when she turned up wearing a mask, but as they were going for a coffee, he knew he was guaranteed some time without that particular barrier. As it turned out, they had cake and her mask came off for longer than he had expected.

But an unexpected preoccupation came over him. As she neatly cut up the cake and ate, he found himself observing the fork as she slid the sections into her mouth, the cream topping occasionally catching on her top row, soon removed by her tongue. As the fork was divested of its load, he noticed the hook-like end of the shortest tine, and it sent a shiver through him. Then it was obliterated as it caught the light and she put it down for a while. She was talking about her interest in modern art and what she liked to see in museums, and he was encouraged by that. Maybe she would relate to his own interest in freer forms of music.

'Actually, I'm also in a band,' she then said.
'Oh, really? What do you play?'
'I sing!'
'What?'
'A kind of jazz, sometimes soul, sometimes even hip-hop.'

'That's quite a mix. Let me know when you play next. I'd love to come.'

There was a pause.

'Ah . . . yes. But an exhibition would be nicer, first.'

'I'll look out for something.'

As their dialogue continued, he thought about his concentration on her fork. They were an unfair match. She could dig away at his tartar with sharp objects and he got pleasure from it, but he could not do that in the same way with her mouth, and he was not about to train to be a dentist. He would have to content himself for now with his regular treatment.

He went back to the Chinese masseuse; she seemed happy to see him again. After the cursory oiling, he wanted to play a bit more, so he asked her if she would put on a mask. He had bought a pack of new masks just in case. She agreed, and there she was sitting in seiza, naked, wearing only the mask. He asked her to slowly pull down her mask and started to examine her teeth, running his index finger along the ridge of her upper row. She looked at him curiously but did not seem put out. She started to pull on him slowly and in turn he explored her teeth even more until he got release. Even after he had come, he started thinking of buying some implements, the kind that had a handle and a short crook. Of course, he would never use it directly, but maybe one day Mariko could teach him . . .

The next time he saw her was at the surgery; she said the cleaning was almost done for half a year. He was almost depressed by this news, and tried to think of some way of prolonging their sessions, but he consoled himself with the thought that he could meet her somewhere on another date.

Eventually, months on, they met at an exhibition of modern art that had come to the National Museum of Western Art in Ueno. The exhibition was a stunning compendium of the best examples of modern art that had come to Tokyo in decades and the show united the two of them to an amazing degree. It did not matter what kind of art they saw. They liked everything, but after a while they did seem to have a mutual preference, and that was for the more angular works, especially for the installations that consisted of objects with sharp points or ridges. And most especially one that was of a splayed, skeletal, rusty figure on its back with its mouth open. Possibly, it represented a person who had been tortured or burned in a fire, or simply some decayed sculptural form that had rusted in the depths of the ocean for many years. It was almost impossible to say if it was a found object or a truly sculpted piece.

It was as Mariko bent over this installation and he moved to follow her inquisitiveness that she did the most startling thing, surreptitiously grabbing his crotch. He had to make a huge effort not to cry out, not really believing she had done this in a public place. But her look confirmed everything.

They left soon after, tightly holding hands. Her grip was almost hurting him.

They sat outside a restaurant in the park for a while waiting for a table, barely saying a word until they got inside. It soon came out.

'I have a boyfriend. He scares me. But I want you. I do.'

'I want you, too.'

'It's deeper than that. He knows about you. He's been following you when you come to the surgery.'

'I don't care.'

Fuck!

'What are we going to do, then?' Yuki blurted.

'Be honest with each other?'

'You mean say what we want to do with each other?'

'Yes, and *to* each other.'

'I've . . . I've been going to a . . . place around here.'

She smiled slightly. Not the reaction he expected. Or was it a smirk?

'I know.'

'You know?'

'He told me.'

'And?'

'It's OK. If you stop now.'

'I was only thinking of . . .'

She placed a finger on his lips to stop him. It excited him beyond what he had a reasonable right to expect.

'Let's go,' she said.

'Where?'

'To your place.'

Then she added, 'By the way.'

'Yes?'

'Do you have a computer?'

Once in his flat, he felt both a thrill and a strong sense of matter-of-factness, almost as if he were arriving home with his girlfriend or wife of many years. But he had never been married and had not had a girlfriend for a long time.

Where to start now? He went for something mundane, offering her tea whilst sitting on the floor.

He would turn on the television soon, if for no other reason than to deflect from the erotic reproductions around the room, all quite tastefully done, some from films such as Robbe-Grillet's *Trans-Europ-Express*, some by established artists such as Makoto Aida with his vision of young naked girls all mixed up in a blender. Inwardly, he had sighed. There had simply been no time to tidy up or re-arrange his place, given the rapidity of events. At least, there was nothing truly perverted on the walls.

'I . . . I'll miss you, you know.'

'No, you won't.'

'I will!'

She burst out laughing.

'No, you won't miss me – because I won't go away!'

'You mean you'll leave him?'

'Yes, and I'll show you what you'll miss till your next appointment.'

While he took this puzzling information in, she reminded him to fetch his computer. By the time he had brought it and set it up on the table, she had produced from her bag a huge camera and several pieces of rubberised plastic or perhaps silicon that looked almost like geometrical experiments in shape. Then he realised that the folds on the plastic parts were actually handles, and everything fell in to place.

Taking off her sweater and deliberately unbuttoning her blouse so that he could see just enough of her cleavage to get him hard, she said,

'Do what I say. You'll like this.'

After motioning him to lean back on the sofa, she asked him to hold the plastic handles so that they hooked into his lips, spreading them so that he made a grimace, not of pain but one that he was sure hardly presented an image of how he truly looked. Standing, she undid her blouse completely and took off her skirt so that she was only in her tights and bra. She pulled gently on him, then left it to pick up the camera. Placing a small mirror inside his mouth, balanced between the plastic sections, she aimed the camera right into it, oblivious of his distorted features, her crotch a gimbal that anchored her whole body and the camera above him. Eventually, she stopped to take off her tights and took his hand, letting him slide it in just enough to harden him more. When she had finished taking the photos, she took out the SD card and put it in the computer.

He was half-expecting that it had all been an elaborate ploy to take pictures of his nakedness and put them on the Internet, but actually she indeed showed him photos of his teeth, going into extreme detail about each one's designation and characteristics – and how best to keep them clean. He did notice perhaps one unintended photo that showed his distorted features, but it was so extreme that he doubted anyone would recognise him from that. But as she showed him the others, she could see that he was getting even more excited, so she pulled on him, eventually taking him in her mouth. With his penis poised over her, then forcing the tip into the narrow spaces between her teeth and the insides of her mouth, the red wall that on the other side was her face, he finally realised that she had a beautiful smile.

'Now,' she proposed. 'What do *you* want to do?'

The Shore

'WHAT ARE YOU reading there?'

Gerald looked across the sand, startled.

He was midway down Waikiki beach between the zoo and the Hilton Hawaiian Village complex, lying on a stretch of sand in front of one of the many beachfront hotels that was open to everyone. The girl who asked the question was simply gorgeous, anything from sixteen to twenty, her hair long and blonde, her turquoise bikini perfectly suiting her pale skin, which had been browned only slightly in the winter sun. For heaven's sake, why would a girl that young start talking to a fifty-year-old man like me on my own?

'Oh, just a crime novel.'

'Crime?'

'Yes, you know, someone is murdered, and the inspectors have to find out who did it, that kind of thing.' From the little he had heard so far, he was trying to do some detective work of his own as to her accent. Possibly Spanish, he thought.

'What are you here for?'

'A conference. I don't have to go to every event.' He didn't know why he offered the extra information, except that she did look like she would be happy to listen to him.

The water was surprisingly choppy, he thought, as he saw a young boy boldly launch himself on a boogie board into the oncoming spray.

'He's brave. I wonder where his mother . . .' As he turned, his unformed question was already being answered, as the mother, a little behind them on the sand, hunched over her mobile phone, wrested her eyes from the device to issue a warning to be careful.

Gerald's new companion saw and heard the same interchange and gave him a knowing look as if she were wiser than her as-yet-to-be-determined years.

She herself had no impedimenta, not even a mobile, which was quite a wonder, he decided.

Then she stood up and walked straight into the water, her calves and the pits of her knees immediately fixing his attention until they merged with the lapping water. She did not come back out of the sea. He lost himself in the book and fell asleep.

He came here from Tokyo every year to the same conference on teaching to get a few tips and to network, but he couldn't remember ever being approached this way before by a stranger. Even though divorced, he was still close enough to make buying presents for his kids a meaningful ambition and a productive way of killing time.

He smiled inwardly as he spotted a young Japanese woman wearing a cold mask as he walked along Kalakaua Avenue holding hands with her boyfriend. But his amusement soon turned to irritation. What in God's name did she think she would catch walking around Oahu? Hopefully, she would soon realise she was about the only person on the island trying to shield herself from airborne germs. At least her companion was giving himself to the sun.

As he walked back slowly along the beach, he could not but admire how unconcerned everyone was about their bodies, with the exception of the show-offy aerobics fanatics in the fitness centre on Kalakaua with their blaring music and the trainer's stentorian instructions, enhanced even further through the PA system, like a direct exhortation to the innocent tourists below feasting on their ice-creams and assorted cream lattes to desist from enjoying themselves. At one stage he could have sworn one guy wearing dark glasses and a white vest was looking directly at him; it was a stern, reproving stare.

As he arrived at the Hilton Hawaiian Village where he was staying, he overheard a unique chat-up line, at least as far as its audacity was concerned. A forty-year-old white American hunk of beefcake in a baseball cap tethering an Alsatian that gazed longingly towards the beach was delivering his line to a young Asian girl:

'You wanna go out?'

Nod.

'Get some drinks?'

Nod.

'I give you my number'.

?

All this was issued in deathless staccato. In Gerald's experience, a nod or even a 'yes' did not necessarily mean a 'yes' as such, however.

Maybe I should try that, Gerald thought. I'll first have to get myself a dog, a proper body, a baseball cap, a tan, a fixed smile, and a deep American accent, though. And maybe some balls, too.

The second day he went on a drive with a Chinese teacher called Amy about twenty years his junior as much to have something to do as for companionship. Through her he had been witness to one of the most startling transformations he could remember. At her presentation she had dressed like a glittering Disneyesque character. By the time she turned up for their drive, she was unrecognisable in straight slacks, a white shirt, untucked, and a formless fishing hat. But she turned out to be an informative and pleasant guide, knowing the island very well. They kept to the coast, jumping out to take the odd photo with the seas as collaborative backdrop.

She seemed to keep her distance a little once she learned he lived in Japan. He probed a little about the Chinese attitude to the Japanese and tried to represent the Japanese in a responsible and reasonable way but she was non-committal. He guessed that she did not want to get into an argument.

One memory from the trip would stay with him for some time. They were eating at a wayside restaurant, a tent with plastic tables and chairs in front of a camper van. A Spanish-speaking family was chatting away; what he took to be the not-quite-middle-aged father and mother were sitting at right angles to each other, forming an L, which two young women, whom Gerald took to be their daughters, mirrored on the other side of the table. They were relaxed, the mother being the most active conversationalist of the four. He had no idea what they were talking about, but he could almost enjoy their good-heartedness vicariously, chuckling to himself when they laughed at a comment. Then, a young girl, perhaps seventeen or eighteen years old, drifted into the picture and sat on the man's lap, turning her head and gesturing to him to scratch her back. She grimaced slightly as he followed orders. The possible father pushed his hands up under her top till they revealed the straps of her bra, then, tentatively, almost regrettably, retreated. The girl demonstrated instant satisfaction but pulled away when he started to nuzzle the nape of her neck, the mother and probably the other daughters all the while oblivious to the intricacies of the exchange.

Gerald felt a mixture of sickness and envy. 'Did you see that?' he said to Amy. 'What?'

'There's no way that guy's her father, surely.' 'I didn't see it' was Amy's only reply.

Elizabeth would never let me do that, he thought, but then his daughter and he had hardly the warmest of relationships.

The next day, a presentation on nuclear disarmament caught his eye. He ended up missing it but arrived in time for the second presentation on climate change by the same speaker and for the discussion that followed. The presentation was so abstract that he wondered for a while if he hadn't stumbled into a parallel conference on some New Age philosophy or even a cult recruitment session. He managed to get in a couple of questions about Chinese militarisation and the recent Russian bomber training missions in the North Atlantic. The genial speaker professed surprise at mention of the arms build-up and the manoeuvres – unless he was just being tactful, given the international make-up of the audience.

An hour later, after a brief chat with the speaker, Gerald was back at the beach, day-dreaming about why he wasn't out there surfing, recalling that there had been a presentation on one woman's debilitating fear of water and her recovery. 'I'm not afraid of the water, really,' he thought. 'I'm just afraid of everything. Well, I was afraid of marrying and having kids, at least. Maybe I still have it in me to be a Mishima, but I'm not keen on suicide. Maybe I'm just not frustrated enough.'

He walked out onto one of the piers on Waikiki, congratulating himself on bringing his sandals. He turned to one side and sat, his legs dangling. A figure edged up wordlessly next to him. He hadn't been aware of anyone else on the pier.

'No book today?' she enquired.

Her skin was right up against his. This time she was wearing a golden-yellow bikini almost the same shade as the sand.

There weren't many Caucasians he found attractive these days. He had long since surrendered to the exotic, slender, tiny frames of Asian females.

'Oh, I'm too restless to read for long periods right now.' Then, he added, 'Aren't you with someone, if you don't mind my asking?' 'My parents are over there. They don't mind.'

He looked over at the beach, following the line of her arm, unconvinced this method was precise enough to locate her parents, his eye drifting in the process across her small chest as if he were an awkward teenager.

'Boyfriend?'

She shook her head dismissively, perhaps regretful in some way.

'Well, you won't be without one for long, I can tell you that.'

From the corner of his eye, he saw small, black crabs sidling across the boulders along the side of the pier.

'Just look at that,' she said, 'I wonder why they are black.'

'Yes, with all these beautiful, bright colours all around us, too.'

'Maybe it's camouflage?'

'On these rocks, yes, maybe it is.'

'Have you ever wanted to disappear like that, into the background?' she pursued.

'Well, you know what Jack Nicholson says in *The Passenger*?'

He received a blank look. ' It's a film.'

'Yes?'

'People disappear every time they leave a room, though not in so many words.'

'So many words?' He chuckled.

'It's just an expression. It's not important.' But she picked up the thread.

'I heard that what we see isn't actually physically coloured the way we see it, right?'

'Yes, I've heard that. I'm no expert, but it's obviously how our brain interprets light coming off certain molecules, or not, as it were.'

'I heard,' she added eagerly, 'that everything is really more or less grey, if we could see how it really is.'

'Yes, it makes me think of black holes. How everything can be eaten up as if it never existed.'

'Black holes scare me.'

'Oh, don't worry. There's nothing to be scared of,' he reassured her, only realising the unintended joke as he enounced it. 'For example, do you know how many people you would have to crush together to make a black hole even the size of a proton?'

'No.'

'10 billion! More than all the people in the world alive now.'

'Ay ay ay. That's crazy.' Then, 'I'm not afraid any more. You've cured me!'

'Happy to help a charming young woman like yourself.'

She leaned towards him suddenly, pecked him on the cheek, then ran off.

He tried to see which direction she was headed, but she soon merged with the beach and then, he supposed, the crowd.

'$50 to the house and then you discuss with woman.' He glided in rather than walked. One could be forgiven for forgetting the sleaziness of the area he had just passed through, a cluster of lonely commercial entities more looking like car parks than shops and businesses.

She was Asian, slim, doe-eyed, diverging little from the photo he had seen on a forum, but now she was dressed in a white romper.

She washed him down in the shower, got him to lie face down on the mattress, and started oiling him. He would only go so far, maybe wouldn't even ask for much more than a little skin contact. He certainly didn't trust any of these places for more than a little rubbing.

At bottom, he did not want full engagement with a woman; he just wanted to look at her and be looked at.

His was a fetish that he could hardly name, a fear that shifted him to an unnameable region that could only be experienced for a short time, as if he were being pushed to the edge of a cliff, dangled, made to long for a descent and demise, then pulled back suddenly to safety.

In reality, the sensation was little more than a need to be touched rather than to touch. All the rest, the images of transgression, darkness, bright lights, fear above all, were decorations around this world, like topping on an ice cream that had disappointed merely by the fact that he had chosen the wrong flavour.

He came out into the semi-gloom feeling like he could taste the different colours of the lights which moved with his steps like the bright, animated illustrations of the atoms of a nucleus. His senses sharpened, the air around him almost achingly clear now, he was, improbably, dissatisfied.

The reptilian eye was perfect in its unblinking, primordial concentration. Keeping his distance as the instructor had advised, Gerald felt nevertheless outside himself. Coming to the surface, he saw the Spanish family on another boat. The blonde girl was wearing a pink outfit this time. She waved to him, then dived in. The father followed her down; neither was snorkelling, unlike him. He swam towards them, then went under for a while when he lost sight of them. Coming up, he saw them about ten metres away, the man encircling her. They had no interest in turtles. He swam as close as he could to them without seeming like a voyeur, dipping under once more, just long enough to see the man slide her bottoms down and reach between her legs. Their bodies turned in the water to keep buoyancy so that Gerald could now see the girl from behind and the man's other hand encircle her buttocks and move a finger into her. Part of Gerald wanted to see more; another part could not bear it.

Back at the hotel, he slept for hours into the evening, his mind full of the scene he had witnessed in the water. He felt a crushing weight on him, as his own body slipped in between the couple's and then out, pulled back and forth by the current; then he was undergoing the more familiar feeling of a sleep paralysis that he often experienced at home. He was aware of something immensely dense pressing on him, which he now saw as a hole in the near distance that was tightening like the pupil of an eye, decreasing in area as it was irised to an unimaginably small point and drawing him around it at increasing speed. By moving a limb, he was able to pull out.

Awoken with a start, he rushed to the balcony of his room. Looking down at the shore from his hotel, he saw the water inundate first the beach, then Kalakaua, and sweep away every person in sight. There had been almost no warning. Very soon, it was lapping at the sides of his seventh-floor room.

He had never been to Pearl Harbor before in all his visits. He really did not know what to expect, having only the most superficial knowledge of the war in the Pacific. As a

Brit, he had no real point of contact for it, and no interest in POW stories, but a casual mention of it in the presentation had captured his interest.

At the wide-ranging Visitor Center he was fascinated by the petrified missiles in the grounds of the museum and horrified by the sheer lunacy of the Japanese attack, an attack that led in a straight line to the bombs of Hiroshima and Nagasaki, in his opinion.

Only the Regulus missile, from what he knew about its role in the Cuban Missile Crisis, meant anything to him. No time to go on the 'boat' or the memorial to the Arizona that still leaked oil.

She was there, of course, in the shadow of her unlikely father, in a red dress with white polka dots hardly fitting the spirit of her surroundings, unless she had stepped out of a party in a New York apartment, circa 1945. The man was photographing her against the dark blue Regulus I.

Gerald seized his chance and went up to them to offer his services for a two-shot. She stood, imperial, holding her father's hand. He didn't seem to speak any English, to Gerald's relief.

He was back to his novel on the beach, nearly finished. Light was fading and the population was swelling slightly as tourists congregated for the sun setting on the horizon as if in search of some revelation.

She was wearing bright orange.

'You have nearly finished?' she said, indicating the book.

'I thought you wouldn't come,' he replied calmly.

She smiled as if to say, You knew I'd be here.

'The man I see you with. He touches you a lot, almost

like a lover . . .'

She lay down, not quite next to him, but at an angle, making an L, so that he saw the fullness of her left thigh and her cleavage in deep foreshortening, emphasising its depth all the more.

She reached out for his hand, pulled him up, demanding they have their photo taken.

'I don't have a stick,' he joked.

She took his mobile and handed it to an Asian woman, who duly obliged.

Behind him, the orange ball of the sun was about to touch the very rim of the sea.

He let his hand fall down her back, and held her bottom gently. One kiss before she walked off?

He did not look at the photo until he was on the plane back to Japan. Her Day-Glo orange bikini had succeeded in merging perfectly with the orangey-red of the great orb, rendering them a unique mass of saturated particles and pixels.

Green to Blue

THEY MET HIM at the main railway station and cheerily put his things in the estate car. Their morose seventeen-year-old daughter was with them; he could not guess why. Only much later did he think to ask himself why she had been there that day. Nevertheless, during the journey to his new lodgings he already felt pampered by their attentions.

Such was their interest, which seemed genuine, that he hardly looked at the landscape. The greenness of landscape bored him, though on this occasion he might have taken notice. It was rather another green that held his attention, that of Miranda's eyes in the rear-view, which wandered from the surface of the mirror to the road in front and finally sideways to her husband, the quieter of the two. Yet there would have been nothing so remarkable about this interplay had he not felt the closeness of that mirror, the projection of the plane unusually towards him.

They were delicate in their questioning. He felt his earlier resolve to hold back weakening, but before he gave in, he managed to divert the conversation away to generalities about the city and their village.

The house was a converted farmhouse. On the way in, they pointed to the separate entrance door to his flat at the side. This door, he was told, led up a set of stairs to the first floor where he had his own kitchen and room. But he didn't want to see that straightaway, surely.

He was guided to a sofa where he was told to relax while they prepared the food. He could not stay still for long. Noticing this, they encouraged him to look around.

The walls were mostly pastel colours, decorated sparsely but tastefully with a framed Ordnance Survey map of the local area, a Persian rug, and a number of photos. All of these were modest in their positioning and colour scheme; even the rug was placed so as to be in permanent shadow, he calculated from the angle of the falling sun. There would have been nothing unusual about this had he not suddenly realised that at the centre of the back wall, where most of these objects were, was an oil painting which he had inexplicably failed to see till now. He gave the picture all the greater attention as a result.

The picture showed a slender, pale, naked woman standing in a dark thicket of jungle. He could not have dated it; he knew very little about such things, but it must have been very old because of the intricate network of cracks. He was almost at as much of a loss when it came to explaining why it captivated him so much. Then the obvious occurred to him. The woman bore a marked similarity to Miranda, especially in her wide, staring eyes, except that the painted woman's eyes were blue.

He felt Michael's presence behind him before it was confirmed by his words.

'You like it?'

'Yes. Did you do it?'

'Heavens, no. We found it in a junk shop. It . . .'

'Looks so much like Miranda?'

'Yes, you're sharp. I really don't know much about this kind of thing. Miranda does, though.'

'You think,' came Miranda's interjection from the kitchen.

Under his breath, and guiding Paul back to the sofa, Michael added, 'She's modest. That's all.'

'Food's nearly ready,' she said as if to confirm his claim.

With a knowing smile, Michael jumped up and went back into the kitchen.

He was tired. The sun was now hiding behind a distant hillock he could see through the window. With no lights yet turned on, the darkness seeped into the room like a dye, and objects began to congregate around him, irrespective of their weight or the fixtures that held them to surfaces. A murmur of voices circled him, then whorled upwards into a distant place.

In his dream Hana placed her arms around him, her breasts supporting his head. He reached up for her but grasped at space. He fell, the loss magnified by the distance, which, like the combined speeds of two crashing cars, shortened itself by coming towards him as quickly as he was going to it.

The clink of glasses must have woken him. When he turned around, he saw the three of them smiling. They looked like a family for the first time. Their plates were empty, their wine glasses were half-full. Miranda said, 'I'm sorry, we tried to wake you, but you were far gone.'

'How long have I been sleeping?'

'Oh, just half an hour. The food's still hot.'

The rest of that evening was taken up with pleasantries. They only discussed a few items concerning his flat when they finally showed him what was to be his home for the foreseeable near future.

They entered his place through a connecting door which went through his bathroom into a small kitchen. There was a key, but as if to reassure him, Miranda said, 'Don't worry, no one'll come through, except to bring in the washing.'

The place itself was small, with rudimentary furniture, a smattering of prints and antiques – small assurances, rather than mere tokens, of their confidence in him, he judged, as a safe tenant, something in no small part due to the recommendation he was sure his new employer had given. He had everything he needed, as far as he could see. There was even a balcony with a cityscape made up of pinpricks of light. He was amazed that this far out they could see the city at all.

He wasn't sure if the door worried him or not. It certainly modified the description of 'self-contained flat' somewhat, but the occasional interruptions would surely have their compensations.

The city could have been any large city in Europe that had trams. Avoiding the quicker but harrowing train ride, he took a bus for twenty minutes, then caught the tram into work. Usually, he got a seat but would vacate it for an old person. At first, he had resented it; the old people were shadow people whose excess of number and presence, weighted down with years and buried thoughts, threatened to swallow him up. Not much later, when he heard of the death of a friend the same age as him, he began to look upon them differently. We fear them, he thought, because they are really us, with our frailties and dreads hollowed out, unburdened; they pity us in turn because they can see those frailties and dreads still residing in us and know the journey we must yet make.

He developed two lives, and worked on them with equal application. His city life was partly characterised by randomness. He would sometimes take a bus or tram without bothering to look at the number or destination; only this way could he discover something new. The city was a brain; it even had a left and a right side, and it was his task to map its paths and neural networks. Sometimes, despite these ministrations, he would find himself standing on a corner, completely unaware of what he was doing in this place. Sometimes he even forgot what his job was.

His second life, which took place in his flat in the country, was less predictable. There was really no connection with the city. It was necessary to invest it with a sense of mystery, to make it a puzzle, and because of his nature and his particular situation, this was not difficult. Reinforcing this separation was his own past; what he had been, where and with whom, these were cemented to the city half of him, and they were external to the man of twenty-nine who went up the stairs of his flat and was sometimes chanced upon by his affable landlady or landlord, though seldom by their daughter.

◊

Contrary to his initial misgivings, none of the family came through the connecting door without first knocking, and even these visits were limited to essential things, which after the first few weeks had been sorted out. Without complaint, Miranda got used to the frequency of the washing he gave her to do, necessitated by the paltriness of his clothing.

He was perhaps a little concerned with the distance the family had shown since that first evening he had moved in. In the course of the following months, he had gone from wanting to maintain his privacy to feeling a need for some contact. He was relieved, therefore, when Michael tapped lightly on his door one Friday evening and invited him to eat with them.

The room had been rearranged somewhat, so that the longer side of the dining table ran along the back wall where the painting was hung. While Miranda passed the food to Michael through a serving hatch, Paul noticed the painting again, slightly to the left of the chair, which was in the dead centre of the wall. Pippa breezed into the room and took her seat just as Michael was passing around the food. Michael sat on Paul's right, and Miranda eventually came through and sat opposite Paul in the chair in front of the picture so that her image seemed ghosted by that of the naked figure.

The customary platitudes were indulged in, the kinds of non-topics he had succeeded in escaping from for some time. Now he was reconciled to the fact that such a reversion was inevitable. But he did not anticipate the acuity with which conversation and incidental detail would be directed at him, and from him to them. Miranda had a perpetual look of amusement on her face when she spoke to him, and this unnerved him a little, but it seemed the correct counterweight to Michael's self-absorption, and Pippa's fixed scowl.

'We still know hardly anything about you, Paul,' Miranda said, pausing. Then, 'I hope you don't mind my asking.'

'No, not at all.' He had to think quickly here. It was the way with him that he could not successfully hide facts; even explaining the simplest embarrassing personal tick of his became a complexly involved circumlocution that in the end revealed whatever he was attempting to mask.

'Well, there's not much to say, really. I've been living abroad for years, mostly teaching, and I'm divorced.'

'Just that?' Miranda's amusement was a dance on a thin surface of ice, he saw now for the first time. 'I'm sure you're just being modest about yourself. You can't say that about everyone.'

Paul thought he caught a quick, electric exchange of glances between her and Michael, but he wasn't certain. 'Of course, people have to keep *some* things to themselves,' she added.

The last of these words coincided with Michael's hand reaching out for the wine bottle and knocking over his own glass. The redness shot across the tablecloth like successive explosions, one nested within the other.

'Oh, Michael!'

'I'm sorry, darling.'

No one said anything while Miranda went out quickly for a cloth.

'Well, I've had enough, anyway,' he said, and burst out laughing as she returned.

The bleak attempt at a joke fell on a flat wall of silence.

'Well, *I* haven't. And *I'm* not the one spilling things!'

She stared at Paul as if for support. He realised that she had already had four glasses, and her speech was slightly slurred. He could not decide how far her chiding was serious and how far it was her playing with Michael's outward show of calm.

Pippa had said nothing since she had sat down, and she now got up and went off without a word. There was no precedent in his mind for it, but Paul felt as if a strip of his skin were being flayed off as she left.

But why should he worry? He could not see himself being invited back for a long time. He felt suddenly desperate to change the subject, though he was not absolutely sure that the subject had ever been declared.

He focused on the painting behind Miranda, on the strangely blue leaves and those enormous eyes.

'That really is an amazing picture you have,' he finally said.

Michael stood up and started to clear away the plates.

'Yes, we bought it years ago when we were students. I'm sure it's a Rousseau, but Michael won't even let me get it valued.'

'It's got sentimental value,' Michael retorted as he went into the kitchen.

'Yes,' she said, laughing at something that must have been an old source of tension between them. 'He always says she reminds him of me.'

'Well, that's what I thought the minute I saw it,' Paul concurred.

'Really? Isn't there a discrepancy there? Have a closer look. Come round.'

He walked around the table and stood in the small space

between her and the painting. In the background, he could hear Michael washing and scraping away at the dishes as if he wanted to remove more than just food.

As he studied the figure close up, he became aware of Miranda's hand lightly touching his arm, where it stayed. He tried to concentrate on the painting, exploring for a while the divaricate veins on the woman's breasts, but this told him nothing.

'It's a disease,' she said, baffling him for a moment. 'They were originally green, like mine.' She laughed. 'The green was made from yellow and blue. The yellow oxidised, leaving blue. If it weren't a night scene, you'd notice it more in the foliage.' She said all this with a kind of Fitzgeraldian melancholy he hadn't noticed in her before.

Michael came back in, and she moved her hand away.

'That's your theory, anyway.'

◊

That night his thoughts turned to the connecting door beyond the kitchen: he saw it now as a rectangle blacker than the surrounding darkness. Whereas before it had come to be a way through, a kind of unacknowledged comfort, it was now a plate shifting against the surface of his thoughts, of his isolation, alternately opening or slipping away. Nameless desires arose, and he was transported beyond himself. At the height of these, a form appeared.

Pippa was standing by the bed. He hadn't heard a sound, and her earlier timidity made it all the more unreasonable. She was so much like her mother. The whole thing made no sense. The darkness of the background pushed her towards him, making her dizzyingly three-dimensional. Then he noticed her belly. She lowered herself onto the end of the bed, sitting astride his extended feet. She gave birth to the baby there and then; Miranda came in when the baby's cries echoed out for the first time.

◊

He climbed the hill and looked at the surrounding countryside, gaining an overall view for the first time. In the distance, the hedgerows of the fields ran into each other like braids of hair, dipping, disappearing and emerging as if through gaps in space. He did not adhere to a Romantic view of the country, nor did he ascribe to it some ill-defined therapeutic properties. Perhaps this was why he was all the more exhilarated, standing up here now. Hana was falling back into the distance, and he was being forced onto a ledge of reason.

'She meant a lot, didn't she?'

How long he had been there he couldn't say, but the voice, and, even more, the words it carried, was solid enough almost to push him down the hill.

'Miranda.' Then, 'It really looks that obvious?'

'Fraid so,' she quipped, then, performing a small caracole, as if suddenly taken by girlish precocity, turned back and held his hand.

He trembled, but let himself be guided over to some rocks where they sat down. She pulled his head towards her and let it rest against her shoulder for some time without either of them saying a word.

They were facing the town. The house was slightly off to the right. From where they were, they could see Michael digging the garden as Pippa emerged from the house and handed something to him. The setting sun behind the house spilled a river of ochre onto the brown roof, deepening the shade of the grass. A thin arm, barely defined, reached out a caress, and for a moment the action seemed to be returned.

'When we met, Michael was always full of plans. He had ambitions to work in the theatre, he was always quoting Shakespeare, but it was never corny. We were in London in those days. He never looked at another woman. Then we had Pippa. We got offers to teach, so we settled down here.'

She said all this with the measured contemplation of someone speaking of a long-past bereavement, her hand playing hopscotch with the gaps between his fingers.

'It was perfect for a while.'

He couldn't understand what she was driving at, but he dreaded some revelation. He prayed she would hold back.

'What about you? You've hardly told us anything.'

'There's really nothing to tell. There's no mystery. We made the decision together.'

She tightened her grip and drew closer. He could almost imagine her twenty years before. She must have been irresistible. Prettier even than Pippa. Only a certain sadness interfered. He was aware of her thin, unsupported breasts touching his arm. Their embrace was awkward, as if they were attempting to detach impeding straps or harnesses from each other which had become entangled. He didn't want it to be like this, but he really didn't know what he wanted. They slid down onto the earth and rolled against each other, their momentum almost taking them down the slope.

They woke in the dark. For a moment, he thought he was in his own bed in the house, but mutual, confirming forays quickly disabused him. He did not know what he felt.

◊

That evening he locked the connecting door, leaving the key angled so that it could not be dislodged even if they had another. What was he afraid of? That he would make that journey or she? They were loud that night, but he could not say whether they were having a particularly engaged discussion or an argument. Pippa was more vocal than usual, certainly; on the few occasions he had heard her like this, he had never been able to tell if she was crying or simply raising her voice to make a point.

He put on headphones and immersed himself in a novel but found himself re-reading each page till he gave up, finally falling asleep. When he awoke, it was two o'clock. He was not quite sure if he had woken from a dream or heard a banging noise. Either way, he now had to empty his bladder.

The toilet was next to the bathroom. As he approached it, he noticed a dull strip of light under the connecting door. More than this, he heard a moaning, followed by the rush of someone down the corridor. There was some whispering, but he couldn't make out anything definite. As he returned, for a moment he wondered if Miranda had tried to come through and been discovered. Back in bed, he suddenly realised what his dream had been about. He had been with his ex-wife in a field playing with their child. He could not identify the place, but worse than this was the fact that they had never had a child.

He managed to avoid crossing paths with any of them for the best part of the following week. He stopped locking the door at night; she did not come through. A few days later, his contact was finally renewed but in the least expected way.

He had gone through to the house to tell someone about a problem with his heater. As always, he knocked first, and thought he heard a murmur. Pippa appeared from her room, and the sound of someone hitting something and a muffled curse followed her out. She was wearing only a thin jumper that allowed a generous outline of her breasts and barely reached the tip of a teasing triangle of dark hair below. His observation of this detail was momentary, as she maintained eye contact all the while he spoke. It was only as he was turning away that he registered for the first time the colour of her eyes, a pale blue so deceptive it had taken him this long to recognise.

The next day, Michael caught him on his way in, grabbing him forcefully by the arm, and his heart sank. He almost blurted out a confession, but he was so nervous that Michael had already said what he had to say before Paul could open his mouth. He was inviting him for a walk in the country at the weekend. Relieved as he was, he still wanted to make excuses, but his landlord's sudden affability, combined with a heavy-limbed presence, forced him to accept. It would probably only be this once, he reasoned.

'Just us, of course. The women're off shopping Saturday,' Michael added.

◊

They walked for three hours with few breaks. Paul hadn't had so much exercise in years. Michael gave the impression that the route he was taking was arbitrary, but this was unlikely. Somehow, it unsettled Paul.

The journey seemed to divide into two parts, each fashioned by Michael's steady commentary. The first part was his elaboration of flora. He knew the name for everything, and his detailed, enthusiastic display of knowledge confounded Paul, who could barely name half the trees he ever saw. He marvelled at one point when Michael shouted out 'marjoram' and leapt across a muddy ditch to kindle in his hand the herb that Paul only knew as compressed leaves. The other part was dedicated to a litany of the ailments suffered by one variety or other of plant or tree.

'They're all diseased,' he said later on, picking up a silvery-blue clump of earth which looked like a drowned plant.

'What makes you so pessimistic?' Paul asked.

'You can tell from the colour alone.'

'No, I mean it's a bit general to say *everything's* dying, isn't it?'

'It's part of my job, but anyway . . .'

He looked off into the distance, as if contemplating whether he should continue.

Paul perceived an injustice somewhere. What did Michael, with his own home, a good job, a beautiful wife and daughter, have to feel so miserable about? Paul thought of how he no longer fitted into city life, how he expected a disaster at every turn. But the country was no solution, either. It was empty. What eventually came out of his mouth sounded neither sincere nor portentous.

'I often feel as if the earth is slipping away beneath my feet, as if there's going to be some god-almighty crash.'

For a moment Michael stared at him as if to check his sanity, then suddenly burst out with a laugh. 'Paul, you *are* a character.'

The jocularity remained around them for a while like a low mist, but when it disappeared it was as if an acrid deposit had settled deep inside them.

They entered a forest and walked along the edge of an empty river. For long stretches, neither said anything, and in places, where it became suddenly dark, Paul felt as if he were on his own and the figure of Michael were the cloaked figure of death he had no choice but to follow. He was breathing hard most of the way, till they reached a peak, and then they half-slid, half-ran to the bottom. After ascending another hill, they emerged onto the ridge where he and Miranda had made love, and from which they could see the house.

Michael sat down on one of the stones where he and Miranda had sat. Paul remained standing, a little nervously. An unexpected mustard sky was sliding away from the town, as if this were infused in a crucible. If there was a calm, it was an unconscious one.

'She's dying,' Michael said finally, his gaze still on the house. 'I should have told you but . . .'

'Who? Miranda?'

'A cancer of some kind. These doctors . . .'

There was nothing Paul could say. Only the pain of his foot striking the stone expressed anything.

Paul knew he would not be able to keep the knowledge of Miranda's illness to himself for long. It was only a question of when he would disclose it. He did not see any of the family for the rest of the day, and almost succeeded in forgetting about them until late in the evening when he was woken by the sound of Michael and Miranda shouting at each other and Pippa crying. Finally, he heard Michael leave, smashing the door shut on the way out. Stretched, projected rectangles rode across the back wall of his room as the car skidded in the mud, swung round, and finally left the yard.

He paced around the room for some time, unable to calm down. Finally, he went up to the door and listened, but it was quiet.

He could not remember eventually settling down to sleep, but he felt what woke him was located in the dream rather than in the house. It crossed his mind that perhaps Michael had returned, slamming the door again, but his car wasn't in the yard. Then he remembered it was something to do with the painting, the penetrating stare of the naked woman's almost cerulean eyes.

Checking first for any sound, he entered their part of the house, proceeding stealthily down to the living room. The painting stood out in the perse moonlight, seeming to exist independently, until his eyes adapted to the rest of the room.

Shivering, he stared at the figure, and might have fallen

asleep standing had not the murmured words not worked their way in between layers of sleep and consciousness.

'Green to blue, green to blue, green to blue,' he heard, like train carriages running over sleepers, as the comparative colours of Miranda's and Pippa's eyes superimposed themselves on each other. He could not have said if he had heard those words in a dream or in actuality, but a snapping sound sent a flash of white across this night vision. He moved quickly back, looking around the room, and only after some time saw the dot-encrusted figure of Miranda in the armchair on the far side.

He squatted down at her feet. She said nothing while he searched in vain for the green in her eyes now, but the near darkness did not allow it. 'Green to blue,' she said finally, confirming his suspicion.

'They've gone?' he said.

She nodded, and her body shook.

He thought of his wife, of the dark, of emptiness, where there were no colours, no sounds, no children.

She took his hand and led him upstairs. They looked into Pippa's empty room. He knew now he would stay.

Neither of them returned, either the next day or in the days after.

The Transfer

I F I HAD told you that I left my wife and children out of guilt for another, to atone for a questionable mistake, a temporary misjudgement of seemingly trivial proportions, you'd probably think I was mad – and I wouldn't blame you. I'd be misleading you a little, but only a little. And I need to get the whole thing down, the words, do it justice, and let you be the judge. (Besides, I am but mad north-northwest.)

It's not as if it's over, the change. You see, there's me, Mark, over here, and there's Jason, over there. And to tell my story I have first to tell Jason's.

Jason was an uncertain entity all along, a gentle American man in his late forties working on his life's work, an obscure Hermetic text, Ficino's *The Asclepius*, about which all I knew at the time was that it had something to do with God, magic and alchemy. (I know more now, it's true.) It was partly his unending delineation of his translating tribulations, his assumption that I knew half the time what he was talking about, with all those gods and rituals – that, and an unceasing interest in culture high and low that bound us. And yet whereas I had a burgeoning family, three young kids when I met him, and another about to be pulled into this world, he had already passed through the married stage, sans kids, and come out the other side. Only, that other side was not a new start, but rather something as intangible as what is – or isn't – on the other side of a black hole. It was as if he had folded in on himself, taking with him everything and everyone that had been dear, and was now moving invisibly among us.

We had met teaching at a university in Tokyo, an American and a Brit whose cultures did not so much fuse as miss each other entirely, like galaxies moving through different planes, leaving each unaffected by the other. That was O.K. by me. But neither did we seek the false common ground of wanting to impose our Western views on those of the Japanese, though it has to be said that neither of us spoke the language well enough to be directly affected by it, or even much frustrated by its seemingly illogical ways.

My initial image of Jason was deceptive and unfocused, like a reflection whose source I was ignorant of. In this reflection he was confidant, taking holidays on his own in Thailand and Cambodia and coming back with mildly intriguing tales of life in the jungles I was envious of. He had been befriended by a tribe at one stage; at another he had been propositioned by two African women in a bar. For my part, I've never ventured anywhere more exotic than Japan, or Hawaii. Gradually, that image sharpened, and small segments fell from the mirror, leaving me to pick them up and piece them together.

'I'm telling you, Mark, I need to get back with her.'

'Her' was Junko. They had been married six years, but when I met Jason, their marriage was dead. They'd been divorced two years but they were still good (platonic) friends. To my surprise. And the friendship was thriving.

'It's the worst thing I ever did, Mark.'

'But you said it was dead, didn't you?'

'I let it die, I guess.'

'Why?'

His attention was snagged by an attractive student passing by. I thought it was his student, but she failed to return his longing gaze. Just over his shoulder, I in turn spied the diving pantyline of another student sitting with her back to us. It was pretty normal for these girls, who wouldn't normally say boo to a goose, to wear jeans just perching on their hips with the lip of their panties riding the denim like a surfer about to fall off her board.

'You know, the other day I saw this woman on the train; she looked at me as if we knew each other, Mark. She had that tightly curled kind of hair. What do you call it?'

'Crimped.'

'Yes, that's a nice word, crimped.'

'Japanese?'

'Yes, and, you know, she looked at me the whole journey. I should have said something to her.'

'I wouldn't regret it too much. You don't pick up Japanese girls on public transport. It just doesn't happen.'

The conversation wasn't untypical, but it possessed the kernel of a later shift towards that reflected image I mentioned.

Jason wasn't bad-looking; if anything, he was young-looking for his age. Really, it was hopeless to torture yourself over a non-existent but perceived affinity with a pleasing face or body like that. But I could empathise. I had lost count of the number of times I had just wanted to go up to a young Japanese woman and declare my love simply on the basis of her looks. I had once joked that the students were so cute that sometimes I felt like bringing in a suitcase and taking one of them home in it.

And where did I stand in all this? I was, if not the Clare Quilty to his frustrated saintlihood (his never worthy, mine never quite perverted enough), then maybe the Humbert Humbert. I was Protestant in name, he was Catholic in practice. I was unable to understand devotion, humility, abasement of myself to some idol; he didn't question it. Yet we never butted heads ideologically, even if he was, as Americans say in that inimitably ugly adoption of the passive, 'conflicted'.

How I obtained sexual pleasure was of no interest to him (and probably even less to readers – porn and looking up girls' skirts, basically, though never those of my students, despite what you may hear of teachers in Japan); how he derived any pleasure other than that he got from his translation work was by the same token of intense interest to me.

And that leads us to the mysterious Junko. That's what I would never really know, or be willing enough to explore except by direct questions. [Though underhand enough to write this?]

'Do you ever notice how they look at you and don't say anything?' Jason said once.

'Who? Girls?'

'Japanese teachers.'

'Which Japanese teachers?'

'It's more a feeling they're not saying what they're thinking.'

'Example?'

'That place we work at on Fridays. This place, too. There's a coldness in the air.'

'We're only part-timers, Jason. They don't have any obligation to talk to us. There's the language barrier, too.'

'I guess you're right,' he said with a dying fall, as if not quite convinced of a perfectly reasonable assumption he knew to be unassailable.

I'd mentioned my affair with another teacher but he hadn't wanted to know the details. I knew he would in any case have been antipathetic to tales of diurnal bondage and spanking. What would be the point in eulogising in his earshot the filigreed stamp of rope on my lover's arms and thighs? The marks faded too soon; what was sunken one minute, making a reddened channel through tissue, was quickly level with the raised contours that had so briefly constructed a glistening fleshy intaglio. Anyway.

But I was more interested after a while in Junko and her hold over mild-mannered and self-effacing Jason. Perhaps that was the paradox. Even before I had met her, an image of her was embedded in my mind's eye. I saw her as a fox-like being, triangular-faced, thin, wiry, insubstantial, almost numinous.

Then one day he just said, 'I saw Junko this weekend.'

'I can never work out if you are divorced or not.'

'We are.'

'But you see a lot of her still?'

He didn't comment, just looked slightly askance at me. He wasn't angry, I knew that.

'I had coffee with that teacher,' he went on, making no attempt at a segue. 'I thought she was giving me a sign.'

'Nice tits?'

'I think I just got her wrong.'

A pause, then, 'Mark, do you think I'm going crazy?'

'I want to see this Junko. Maybe it'll help.'

'How?'

'At least I'll have some idea of what she's about.'

We met in a crowded Starbucks in Shibuya, a vortex of Japanese youth and all its affiliated fashion crosscurrents. The coffee shop, all crowded seating and plate glass, looked down on a four-way pedestrian crossing which always reminded me of a St Andrew's Cross, but its purpose seemed to have more in common with the displaced logic of an Escher etching or, maybe, a story by Borges. Sometimes I was sure that some who entered the swarm to cross the junction never reached the other side. Perhaps they ended up in another part of Tokyo in another life with no idea of how they got there; perhaps they were absorbed by the spirit of Mount Fuji; maybe some roamed the shrines and temples of Nara and Kyoto.

She turned out to look startlingly similar to my projection of her, which was thin and birdlike, but I was more intrigued by her rapport with Jason. They weren't exactly twins in the physical sense, but in spirit and gesture they came from the same egg. Whatever shape her body made, it seemed echoed by his. If she arched her back backwards, he might happen to bend forwards to reach something at the same time, doubling and inverting her outline; if she leaned to one side, he might incline his head in parallel with hers. I could not help but think of the lovebirds in Rod Taylor's car as he rounded the hairpin bends of Bodega

Bay in Hitchcock's film of avian frenzy, how they pointed their little heads and bodies in complete synchronicity in the same direction, like twin compass points.

To some, this might imply Jason and Junko were oddballs. Maybe they were at a slight tangent to everything around them, coming in on the action of time a few million nanoseconds late, or even early, like near-identical versions of themselves spilling over from the bubble of a parallel universe into this, then slipping back just as quickly.

It's a long preamble, but that's the point to a preamble. I can't remember a word of what we talked about while she was there, unlike with my other conversations with Jason. Perhaps I sense a neutralising quality in her, negating, even, or 'addicting', an irksome transmutation of the otherwise perfectly serviceable 'addictive'. I now think what I took away from that meeting was both a sense of horror that I might ever see her again and a desire like a strong arm around my throat dragging me back to be with her again. I'm not saying it was sexual desire or compulsion. It was magnetism (by turns repulsion and attraction), gravity, a delayed suicidal will to implode. How else do you explain the urge to look on at a disaster or misfortune, whether it's people jumping to their deaths from towers, people scarred by acid, or burnt in an explosion?

A number of years went by. Jason was deteriorating. He was talking of leaving, going back to America.

I have no intention of misrepresenting my friendship with Jason. I didn't want him to go back, but what had been a seam in the rock his life had been built on, living here with Junko, having given up everything for a soulless part-time existence, along with turning his back on a career in the States (I couldn't say the same for myself), became a widening fault line.

'I'm between a rock and a hard place, Mark.' Scylla and Charybdis? 'Junko won't have me back. I'm too old to get a secure full-time job. And there's no way to get a woman out here.'

I had once popped into the campus library and left Jason outside on a bench. When I came back five minutes later, a dumpy, short-sighted mature student in her mid-twenties had attached herself to him. It took fifteen minutes to shake her off.

I did not see Jason's place until I had known him for a good five years. He lived on the outskirts of Tokyo in one of the clusters of shops and buildings that is called a 'town' in Japan in a flat that was more like the kind of house that in London is divided into separate, anonymous units by Indian landlords. But once inside Jason's den, there was something quite pleasing about the layout, which consisted of a central room immediately inside the front door and two adjacent rooms on the far side. All three had views of the main street, which meandered down from the train station. Jason complained that it was too loud at night, mainly due to the local youths who hung out at the fast-food restaurants a few doors down, but I thought that at least you couldn't be lonely in a place like this. Despite this, and the bewildering assortment of tapes, CDs and books stacked against the walls, on window sills, and on makeshift shelves, it lacked a presence. For whatever reason, I did not think of Junko's old place in his life, where she might have lived with him, so I was astonished when I learned after several visits that this was where they had lived together all their married life. I shouldn't have been so surprised; it's well-known space is at a premium in Tokyo. I just hadn't been able to see it as anything other than a bachelor pad.

'I could get back with her,' he said on one of my visits towards the end.

'What? Things looking up?'

'A bit.'

Looking around his place, I think I was drawn to it by the similarity of its layout to my own flat in Prague. Few days go by without my thinking about that haven a short walk from the local train station; a mere twenty minutes after venturing out, I could be in the centre of Old Prague. Then, after a night of cheap, beautiful beer in my favourite *pivnice*, and hopping from one disco to another, I was safely ensconced in its enveloping anonymity. (Equally, any number of buses would take you to the heart of the Bohemian countryside, where you could be stranded all night if you were unlucky.) But it was in that flat that a number of girlfriends stayed and with whom I singularly failed to sleep, with the exception of my beloved Anneliese.

All my life I have been attracted to small, enclosed buildings, buildings whose rooms slide into one another like nested boxes. In the case of Jason's flat, the two main bedrooms had no doors, just curtains (the one remaining feminine touch?), and the dividing wall, which served as a common jamb and emphasised their twinned state. You could stand in front of them and imagine two lives symbiotically mirroring each other, yet Jason's room (the one he preferred to sleep and work in) and his life as it was now left the question of when the two had ever coalesced.

He stood in the door frame of the preferred room and said, 'Mark, I don't really know if I am going to make it, you know.'

After many months of mental to- and fro-ing, mostly regarding the bills he would leave unpaid if he left before the agreed date, it had got to the point where I was advising him to go back. It was ripping me apart, but I had no choice. If he felt he had no future here, and he was still being rejected by Junko, who at the same time had a grip on him like a black hole on a dying star, it must be better for him to leave.

In the event, he left suddenly, behind Junko's back, an act I fully endorsed. As a favour, I was to take the keys to Junko, and tie up any loose ends, although she would have to do the same with the Japanese landlord.

Somewhat trepidatiously, I made my way to his flat imagining it would be the final, possibly hairy, chapter in what had been a painful separation. I don't know where it came from, but on the way I had a vision of those two adjacent rooms inhabited by two figures I did not recognise.

She didn't say much to begin with, just busied herself making tea. Sometimes, though, as she moved about the room, I sensed a fluttering quality to the light, perhaps a disturbance of invisible waves or membranes around us, that in some way her movements reached into something of the remaining light; but perhaps it was as mundane as her simply blocking the already fading sun.

'He's gone then, flown the coop.'

'The what?'

'The nest. Home. Here,' I said, suddenly aware of a potential faux pas.

'We used to live here, you know.'

'Yes, Jason told me. What are you going to do with his stuff?'

'Keep some of it. I'm not bothered.'

'What about the landlord?'

Oh, that's no problem now. I'm going to move back in.'

'Here?' I said, almost shouting. What was her motivation? Nostalgia? Convenience? Or was she nursing a hope he might come back?

'You know how guilty he felt, don't you?' I said.

'Guilty, why?'

'For divorcing you.'

'Divorcing me? I divorced him! Silly man.'

I was about to protest, but thought, What's the point? How can you know what really goes on between a couple?

'There is a way,' she said.

I had to leave it a moment, to be sure I wasn't hallucinating. I did only think that last thought, not say it? I asked myself.

'Yes, you did, don't worry,' she interrupted.

'You can read my thoughts?'

'Sometimes. It depends on the conditions.'

'What, the atmosphere?'

'Kind of. And feelings.'

I thought, No wonder Jason was so fucked up, with this tugging at you all the time. I looked at her, suddenly realising she could probably read even these thoughts.

She was wearing cord trousers and sitting on the floor with her legs open, a pretty unusual posture for most tight-kneed Japanese women. It was impossible for me to repress my typically invasive thinking.

'What am I thinking now, then?' I challenged.

'You're thinking that I'm small and there's one point between my legs that's small, infinitely small and you want to lose yourself in it. Ah, now you're thinking about those tantalising dips behind the knees of young schoolgirls (why are you thinking about that now?), those blue-grey tendons that flash out at you from time to time and that you want to stroke so much, about those purple knees, purple from the weather, from exposure, from all that rubbing against the plastic mats in sports classes, those pale thighs just a little further up that you ache to touch . . .

'And me. I'm the body that you want to bend, to whip blue, but I'll also suck you in, become you.'

'I can't do that to Jason, you know. I certainly can't do that to my family.'

But in the end I had no answer. She pulled me in. And so here I am, enclosed within her flat, within her arms, within my own mind, sucked up by her, in fact. I have no idea what my wife thinks, that I have left her, been murdered, run away to England. Junko allows me pen and paper, but not access to a computer. That's under lock and key. In fact, she's taken to being my amanuensis, although in truth I am writing for her. She allows me this indulgence, but my main work is to continue Jason's translation, which I labour over most hours of the day and which she then types up. Her reasoning is that if it wasn't for me Jason would still be here working on it but as he is gone, he can't.

But she rewards me at the end of day – or tortures me – by pushing my face into her sticky cunt, which I have to lick until her juices, which are viscous and acidic, trickle down. Then bed, night, inside her. Slowly but surely. I am becoming Jason, paying for his guilt as well as mine, his sin, punished and forced to enjoy at the same time. In my sleep, often when I am in her, forcing all my being into her tiny rank hole, I hear that strange fluttering sound and I think I am being lifted up by an angel. But then I am dropped almost immediately. This is my purgatory, for letting Jason go. This. Simply. Is.

Family Tree

I HAVE NEVER been keen on families. If I could put it down to one event, I would, and perhaps I shall try to do so by the end of this reminiscence. I do not want to say that I am bitter. I do not want to make you feel sorry for me. But here I am, a man in his seventies still coming into his handkerchief, as if after all this time I have not learned anything. Well, perhaps I haven't.

There are probably worse places to grow up in than south London, but its effect is beguiling. Over the years it has crept up on me. I had thought I had long consigned its influence to a distant past, locked it up in a box, and put countries and a continent between it and me. But for some time now I have been aware of the images returning. And they always begin the same way. When I think of our old house now, the house I grew up in, it is always dominated by one scene, one single event. But that will come later.

She is standing at the window, pushed up against the glazing-bar, arms spread, cruciform. Her sidereal presence. Voices urge and reprimand at the same time.

Our new neighbours' three sons – one my age (ten), called Simon, the other two, Michael and John, one and two years older, respectively – knock on our door and introduce themselves. One sits on the low fence running round our front garden, the other is slumped on our dustbin, and the oldest stands, arms crossed. They are placed there like three ascending chimney stacks.

The more I think about it, the more I realise that they were there to assess, to collect ammunition for a battle I could never have predicted was in the offing so early. In fact, it could have been with any other boy my age, with any other family. It turned out later that they had a younger sister, but I would see little of her in the coming years.

My back room gave on to a rank garden set like a brick in a trapezium-shaped block of gardens enclosed by two streets at either corner and a shorter street parallel to ours. The whole back view, in its chaos, sometimes recalled a demented face, like an Arcimboldo portrait, made up of jumbled objects: garden tools for eyebrows, vegetable patches for eyes, the angled, distant projection of a pigeon shed for a nose, and a green-wire fence for a mouth. It was by turns mocking, and threatening. I think already then it knew something I didn't. After all, it could look into the Pattersons' windows.

Soon after moving in, my father and I had cut the back-garden growth down to a decent length, mown it, and built a shed, impinging slightly on the face, but not enough to encroach significantly on its leer. Otherwise, I spent most of my time outside school riding or fixing my bike, making and riding go-carts, and playing in the streets with gangs.

Mercifully, the brothers had decided long ago that the gangs were beneath them; even the idea of leading any of them was probably unexciting. They had, after all, their own gang, with its own implicit power structure, where all the rules were already known. They had the most economical, mutual set-up: blood. It motivated everything, paid for everything, explained everything. I often had the feeling they were just toying with me; what they did with me was a preparation for something much grander.

They are leaning out of their sister Mandy's window, a look of wide-eyed mischievousness discernible on their faces. But I am blind to it. I am fixing the axle on my go-cart, the kitchen door is open, my mother unconcernedly does the washing-up, then brings me a mug of tea.

Michael shouts out, 'Hey, is it true you're a pooftah?'

I didn't know what they meant by this, but I felt that whatever it was I didn't want to be associated with it.

My mother hears this, and says, tolerantly, 'Why do you say that?'

'We just heard, that's all.'

'Well, don't say things like that. It isn't true, anyway.'

THE FINE ART OF WORKING-CLASS TEAMAKING

A typical scene. My mother stands pouring the tea, her flat-footed, unassuming stance somehow indicative of her state, or our situation.

She tips the teapot back. When she resumes pouring, I see a jet of golden-brown liquid darken slightly.

'Why do you do that?' I say.

'Do what?'

'Tip the pot back like that?'

'Habit, I suppose.'

'It makes it stronger if you do that'

'Don't matter.'

'It does. I don't like it too strong.'

Till this moment, my father, quietly checking his pools forms and betting slips, has said nothing. He intervenes.

'Will you shut up? Getting on my nerves.' This to my mother.

'I didn't start it,' she says back.

'Just leave it, will you.'

A silence awhile, and he settles back to the vertical and horizontal intricacies of his *Littlewoods* forms. It's a Saturday afternoon, four o'clock. *Grandstand* is a low hum in the corner of the room. The stakes are high at this time. On top of the racing results and half-time football, wrestling is coming up soon.

'It's not fair,' comes my mother's refrain. 'You always have a go at me.'

The familiar pattern asserts itself. First my mother complains, as if setting a theme. I respond with a counter subject. My father tells her off, ignoring me. From that moment, everything is a variation on a theme that spirals out of control through increasing loops of absurdity, but somehow the whole always manages to return to the original theme.

This is the point at which something HAPPENS. When it does, it always comes as a surprise, though we have been sensing it constantly.

Family Tree

From somewhere near my father – I have never managed to capture that initial moment, that first action – a whoosh issues, and the contents of a cup of tea write themselves across the opposite wall, the dark brown tea only slightly darker than the smoke-impregnated cream wallpaper. I flinch momentarily, my mother ducks, hands on ears. Silence. I take my leave.

Upstairs, reading my first serious novel and masturbating by turns, I listen to them row; it has gained the familiar rhythm now, after that abrupt caesura when the teacup had made its journey across the room. Thus ends a typical summer holiday's day.

Night is another matter. Two rhythms dominate. One is only too familiar and predictable. My father's powerful snoring is accompanied and sometimes interrupted by my mother's complaining counterpoint. This usually, but not always, results in a violent response which manifests itself as a thud, like a boxer hitting a punchbag. Altercation may follow, but not for long.

The other, subtler, rhythm is more disturbing, more insidious, all the more so in that its cause is a mystery. It has something of the sound of material being grasped by hands, material not quite tactile enough to yield to purchase. There are sighs and gasps, but the rhythm is irregular, it falters. The source is unambiguous; it comes from the neighbours, from the wall I share with the girl's bedroom.

In my mind, I try to devise methods of finding out. A periscope-style contraption that I can stick out of my window and point into the room. A mirror placed on the clothes pole at the end of the garden angled so as to allow a powerful telescope to tell all. But my mind, overoccupied as to how I could possibly buy or construct any of these inventions, drifts off. Somewhere, on the further shores of these preoccupations, I hear a high-pitched sound, indefinable but grating. I slip back, my thoughts already overburdened.

In a shop today I was given a sweetly fragrant deodorant, a tester; it aroused me, sexually, to myself.

As the months went by, I began to have hope that I would be admitted to the household's secret indirectly. The brothers became inexplicably friendlier. My father and theirs started chatting over the fence. They even went betting a couple of times.

I took the brothers to my favourite play area, a wasteland by a railway siding next to a crematorium and cemetery. I showed them the bunker I had constructed with corrugated iron, old tyres, and crates. It commanded a view of the whole area. From there you could see who was being buried locally, who was crossing the bridge from another part of the suburb, and even who was making the journey from and into London. Miraculously, the bunker had remained untouched ever since I had made it.

The time I went up there with them was the first and the last. Surprisingly, they brought Mandy along with them. She seemed concerned over little else but the doll she dragged along in the dirt. I thought how much it resembled her, with its Belisha-beacon orange hair, its staring, unseeing eyes, its fixed, reprimanding expression. And yet I knew there was the promise of beauty in her.

They all seemed suitably impressed, but soon lost interest.

They were more set on doing some kind of mischief that I could not guess at. Whatever they were planning was encoded within language alien to me, mixed in with stories about the boys at their school they intended to beat up, three-to-one, the gangs they were thinking about encountering, and each brother's latest inflated sexual experience.

After sending their sister off to play with her doll, as if I had been the one to bring up the subject, they asked me about how I had done in that particular area. I felt no need to lie or exaggerate; after all, there was nothing to exaggerate.

'I haven't done it yet,' I said flatly.

'He's shy,' John said, mocking.

'I heard you and Trace over the road were alone together a few times,' Simon added.

'That's rubbish, I don't even like her,' I pleaded.

'It must be difficult being an only child,' John pursued.

'I like it,' I said, more for the sake of contradicting him.

'You like boys, don't you?' John again.

Without thinking, because it seemed an innocent question, I said, 'Yes. I like you, you're boys.'

My words were met with derisive looks from the other two while John looked on with the affected concern of a parent. 'I told you,' he whispered to them.

'You must like girls,' Simon said. 'Don't you like Mandy?'

'She's nice,' I said.

The older brothers seemed taken aback by this last question, as if it were unauthorised, taboo.

'Don't try anything with her,' John said to me, raising his voice. Shame-facedly, Simon wandered off towards Mandy, who was playing with her doll.

'We saw you looking up her knickers,' Michael added to reinforce John's words. But this seemed to take the game too far. Without turning around, John shot out his fist into the side of Michael's face, leaving his lip bloody.

Michael seemed on the point of tears. At this moment, John turned to look for Mandy. He saw her standing on Simon's shoulders, and shouted out, 'Stop it!'

Mandy jumped down instantly, landing gracefully, and came over to take his hand. The four of them left me there, Michael muttering curses under his breath all the while. I was not quite certain if they were directed at me or his brother.

They did not go straight home. They walked in the direction of the railway bridge, each with an object in their hands, a brick, a bottle, a stone. From my hideout, I watched them as they tried unsuccessfully to vent their familial anger on the next train that came along. The brick hit the roof of the train and bounced back. There was an audible sigh of disappointment, then they sprinted back, taking the path that led around the wasteland.

Sometimes, when the weather is particularly bad, I go out to the local level crossing and take pot shots at the smiling faces in the passing trains.

The next day I went back to the bunker on my own. It had been destroyed, in so far as a hole in the ground with an iron roof can be. To add to my ostracisation, they stopped speaking to me, though, curiously, their father did not seem to bear me any grudge. I remember him a few days after that day on the wasteland talking to my father while I stood at my father's side, as he recited some kind of paean to the family unit.

'There's nothing more beautiful than a family, a loving family, don't you think, Mr Henderson?'

My father readily agreed, though I knew he considered him to be a dubious character. A few days after that, Mr Patterson reinforced and heightened the dividing fence without explanation. I felt strangely comforted by the action, but I was unable to decide whether he was doing it to protect his flock from hostility from outside or to keep their own hostility in.

The pigeon fancier, whose garden adjoined both our garden and the Pattersons', looked on curiously, abruptly turning away from our neighbour's Medusan stare as they made eye contact. I complimented myself that I at least was able to look him straight in the eye. I went upstairs, played my T. Rex records and fantasised about Marc Bolan.

The sounds from the neighbouring room went away for a while, but returned after a few months. They started to intrigue me again, but I despaired at ever now discovering what was happening. Then, coming back from school one day, I was elated to find out that the council had deigned to grant extensions to the kitchens of all the houses on our block.

For me, this did not signify so much the promise of much-needed extra room in our pre-War terrace as a major opportunity to get to that window with relative ease.

It took six months before the extension was finished, but by that time I had almost lost interest. I no longer heard the sounds so often. There would be no point in running the risk of being caught if nothing were going on in there. Besides this, I had started secondary school, a different one to the brothers', and I was immersing myself in homework every night. Little could distract my thoughts, not even my parents' fighting or the prospect of chasing after girls.

Then, one Saturday, when it was nearly dark, I heard a familiar sound coming from the garden as I lay on my bed. At first, I thought it must be coming from the room next door, but instinctively I looked out of the window. The three brothers, to the backdrop of that burning nummary disc in the sky, were in the process of performing a balancing act, the two younger ones supporting the oldest. John, perched pyramidally on their shoulders, was looking out at the gardens as if surveying a battlefield.

I seem to remember feeling slightly nauseous. Where it came from exactly I cannot say. Whether it was the sight of John's amber freckles creeping salamander-like over the pale skin of his back, a sense of utter meaninglessness that suddenly came over me, or the sight of the parents standing at the back door looking on approvingly, I cannot say, either. Then, the unexpected happened as John turned towards my window. I backed off a little: I was confident he couldn't have seen me behind the net curtains, but I was always especially careful. Then I realised that he was not looking over at my window, but the one next door, Mandy's. Peacock-fashion, he shouted out, 'Hey, Mandy, look at this.' A weak, tremulous cry of appreciation followed, and John jumped down without warning, digging into one of his brother's shoulders as he did so. 'What a family', I heard the father say as they all went in.

Family Tree

She is standing there, the fire blazing in the panes, supporting her, making her body into a shifting surface of hell. Is she burning now?

Things deteriorated even more. One day I was called to the front door to face a summary court set up by the brothers, their mother, and their little sister. I had been out cutting the hedges most of the morning. The mother produced Mandy's doll. A series of thin, eyelet cuts ran up both arms like chevrons. Obviously, nothing short of heavy-duty scissors or shears could have produced such an effect, they declaimed in varying degrees of articulateness. My mother defended me forcefully. Never doubting that I hadn't done it. I hadn't, but in the clan's eyes I was found guilty and convicted. They never carried out their punishment except through a continual, baiting harassment. Perhaps they realised how farcical it was, suspecting that one of them must have done it, and they were unwilling to accuse each other. The whole charade had just been some kind of cathartic ritual for them. A little while later, the same family's head launched a nocturnal assault on my father, for another dubious motive. I did not retreat away from the world as a result of any of their tricks; it just made me wary and reawakened my curiosity.

Another summer passed, and thoughts of the family were as distant as the life I would one day lead. I rarely saw them, but when we did cross paths, there was no outward belligerence. I was still haunted by the thought that there was something unspeakable that could have happened to me that time we were out on the wasteland. I hadn't noticed the landscape of the place at the time, but since then it has returned constantly like a slowly developing photo, a greyish swirl of shapes cast in crimson light, a gallows landscape.

The night I saw into their house for the only time was after that mild, indifferent summer. It was on Guy Fawkes Night. My parents were unusually in harmony; ours was a proper family for once. My father and I gathered all the wood we could, and I inhaled the smoke dizzily, daring the flames to grow ever higher to engulf the whole terrace, but at the same time terrified that any harm should come to us. My mother prepared potatoes for baking.

From the back door, ours and the competing brothers' bonfires now seemed like the hellish burning eyes of that monstrous face that haunted me by day. There was no ill-will coming from the Pattersons, for once. We even shared food and drink. But in one area nothing had changed. They still would not let Mandy down into the garden, as was the case every Guy Fawkes Night. As ever, she had to observe the proceedings from the window, standing there against the bars in her nightgown, the reflection of the bonfire painting on her white gown a sea of fire, as if she had been put to the stake.

The mother and father got particularly drunk that night. They went in quite early, shortly afterwards, as did my parents. I was left to poke around at the embers of our fire, while the brothers huddled together debating something. Eventually, they went in, saying nothing.

I sat on the step of our back door in the hope of seeing a few last-minute fireworks. There were a few, but not enough to hold my attention. Exceptionally, I had been allowed to have some wine.

I fell asleep. I do not know what woke me. Perhaps it was a rocket, but I remember no flash. Or a scream.

A familiar sound made its way to me, crawling along paths I had thought long closed. I looked up and saw the reddish glow in Mandy's room. The window was open. Once more, I heard the rhythm that had mixed in it the kind of sound that is itself completely mundane but, amplified, runs along the edges of one's teeth like chalk on a blackboard. I could ignore it no longer.

There was enough room on the window ledge of our extension to allow me to lever myself up onto the roof. As I crawled along, the sound was clearer but no more revelatory.

When I looked into the room, what I saw made no sense. The room was larger than I had imagined. After a while I realised that what was in our house three rooms was here one room, and the ceiling had been raised into the attic. This could only mean that no one in the family had a separate bedroom, unless they were downstairs, which was unlikely. But these observations were fleeting, and secondary.

I was captivated by the shape I eventually made out.

It was that of a tree. The father, mother, and John formed the base. Spanning their shoulders, Michael and Simon made up the second level. On their shoulders, like an angel on a Christmas tree and somehow displaced by her size and innocence, was Mandy. They were all naked.

Here, without my being able to rationalise what was in front of my eyes, was the shape, in its most concrete form, of the spectre that plagued me and still plagues me. I wanted to be sick, but I was too fascinated. They kept up this strange configuration for ten minutes. Then, after slowly dismantling themselves, they sat in a circle. The father, and each brother, took turns to enter the unprotesting girl, while the mother encouraged. At this point, I slivered down under the window and crawled back to my own window, where I was pulled into my room by resources I thought had deserted me.

For years afterwards, I managed to convince myself that it was a nightmare. Nothing in the bearing of the family immediately after that night betrayed any sign that anything significant had happened. And perhaps I would have succeeded in this delusion had I not stumbled ten years later on an article in a newspaper which reported the discovery of a young woman's body on the wasteland where I used to play. A quick call to my father was enough to confirm the woman's identity.

I was at university then, and in a fruitful, satisfying relationship with my first and only girlfriend. We broke up shortly afterwards, and I have never attempted to regain that sense of harmony. I could never, while the image of that young girl continues to burn itself into the screen of my recollection.

The Folding Man

H E WOKE FROM a disturbed night's sleep, having felt a certain kind of oppression, as if a body were smothering him. He had not had one of his sleep paralysis events for a while now, that feeling of someone being in the bedroom other than Kate or their daughter Pippa, who at her age sometimes came in to escape a nightmare.

No, this was more a sense that something, or someone, was enveloping him, but he could not say whether there was in this presence in the room a malevolence or an attempt to comfort him. He realised he was sweating, a lot. Kate was unruffled, oblivious to what must have been his twistings and turnings, as evidenced by the torque in the bedsheets, as if he had been parachuted into his bed and the oneiric harness had been pulled in every direction by a powerful wind.

Downstairs, Pippa was practising her origami. At the age of five, she, like many children, had much more facility with activities that to many adults seemed as complex as designing a jet engine. What was she trying to make? he asked. It wasn't the customary crane.

With a slight swivel of her neck, as if deliberating a

matter of some weight, she said, 'Daddy! Can't you see it's a damsel fly?'

'A damsel fly?'

'You don't mean a dragon fly?'

'Nooooooo. They're way too scary, and, besides, the wings are held differently.'

'Well, you are a clever one. Who taught you that?'

'Mummy, of course!' she clarified, as if she could not understand his bafflement at her precocity.

At some point he became aware of Kate looking through the open door to the kitchen. At least, he assumed she had been standing there looking on; otherwise, he was sure that he would have noticed her in mid-step on her way in.

She put an arm around him almost at the same time as she delivered an affectionate twist of her hand across the top of Pippa's head. She was wearing her favourite indoor cardigan, and he liked the feeling of being squeezed between its openings onto her full chest.

'We gotta go, handsome.'

'Awww,' Pippa let out, almost as if echoing how she thought he might feel at this news.

'What time will you be back?' Kate followed up.

'I guess around 8:00?'

'Going to that place again?'

'Massage? Yes, straight after the office.'

She was still holding on to him, slightly swaying.

'Everything O.K.?' he asked.

'Yes, absolutely. Everything's fine.'

No sense of irony, he thought. The way he liked it.

Feeling he had earned a rest after an unmemorable day

at work, he went for the massage he had awarded himself nine hours in advance. Massage for him was a solace, a way to switch off in a way he could with no other aspect of his life. To be sure, it was sensual, not sexual. In the area he frequented, there were many such operations. It had taken some while to find the right one which was a bona fide business – and a masseuse to his liking. What was special about this place was deceptively simple. The tables were not just flat tables with an oval hole in one end to allow you to place your head straight down; they were padded in a way that at first did not look inviting at all, as if someone had thrown large cushions on a sofa willy-nilly and then laid a cover over them. But they were positioned in such a way as to accommodate the body, to soften and support it in a style rarely backed up in reality by anything even advertisements for comfortable mattresses usually claimed. For once, you could sink down into them without fear of suffocation.

He didn't care which particular oil was proffered to him. It really was mumbo-jumbo as far as he was concerned, except for the sincere intention behind its application. They usually played Keith Jarrett, or something similar, light piano music more often than not, the kind of music which layered chords and notes one on the other rather as the masseuse herself overlaid waves of touch and oil.

It had taken him many visits to many different parlours to reach this state of present satisfaction. Sometimes he would even book a different girl in the same parlour, almost to confirm there was no one better, and indeed it only served to remind him of all the times he had never been totally happy.

Other times, he would fall asleep for the majority of a session, and he would feel cheated. But this could be outweighed by being left on the table after he had been woken to say his session was up, only to slumber a little longer with the persistent feeling that he was still being massaged. He had the sensation of a ghostly continuation of the masseuse's ministrations.

But what fascinated him more than anything was something that had seemingly little to do with the main reason for his visits. It was a kind of puzzling-out of a process that he could not see directly, and in essence something quite banal: the arrangement of the towels which were used to cover him. More significantly, this process was accompanied by the feeling that he was disappearing, perhaps in increments during any given visit, or perhaps it was the accumulated experience of all his visits.

Now, common sense, and plain decency, told him that his bottom half was covered with a towel, and she would work her way up his legs under it as he lay face down. This would last about ten minutes but felt more like thirty. Then, the towel that covered his back would be folded down, doubling the layer on his lower half, and he would enjoy an upper-body massage.

Next, he would be turned over to lie face-up, his body covered anew from head to foot, his upper half being slightly raised by the mechanism under the table so that his waist felt like it was hinged. If a mirror had been placed at the end of the table, he imagined his body would have looked unnaturally foreshortened, as in a Rembrandt painting he had once seen. And not wanted to see again, for that matter, because it showed the partial dissection of a corpse's body, exposing the subject's stomach and brain. The latter, as he remembered, gave the dead man, who could otherwise have looked alive, from his docile expression, the appearance of having a tumescence of red plaited hair.

The towel covering his lower half was folded up enough to cover his mid-section. Again, she would oil his legs and slightly inside his thighs. It was at this point, where exactly he could not say, that he felt himself being compressed down towards, if not indeed folded over onto, his lower half.

His customary visits did not diverge from this basic repertoire, and it was in this way that today's massage went ahead. What was never quite the same, of course, was what was in his head, what he thought about, what had led up to his visits in the days or weeks before, in his life. But these cerebral events were soon forgotten, neutralised by the pleasantness of the massages.

When he arrived home, Pippa was shrouded within her blanket, foetal-positioned, encased in a dome of YouTube films. Kate, at the kitchen table, was similarly tied umbilically to her iPod, Facebooking, as far as he could tell. On the windowsill of the living room was Pippa's old damsel fly, perfected over the years until it had become emblematic of her childhood obsessiveness and physical dexterity. And much larger. Out of the corner of his eye, he sometimes mistook it for a model WWI plane.

In fact, at only thirteen, she seemed quite determined to be a model-maker, taking her earlier natural fascination with doll's houses and mannequins to a more ambitious level, moving in the direction of miniature reconstructions of places from history. It boded well for an interest in anthropology, architecture, or possibly even in set design.

'How was your massage, darling?' Kate asked over supper.

Pippa was eating methodically, efficiently, within herself, as if to give the impression that this was her exclusive focus. Sometimes she pushed a vegetable or section of meat to the side as if to create a border between herself and her parents.

'Oh, you know. If it stays the same, I'm not complaining.'

What was it now? Six, seven years? With the same masseuse.

'We went to the park today. Pippa was off.'

'Oh, nice. Find anything good?'

He directed the question at his daughter, who was staring straight ahead, except that she seemed not to be looking so much at her mother as into a pocket of space between them. Was she resentful at the recent embargo on not using their mobile phones at the dinner table? The habit had recently crept in with all of them. But then, what happens when you take it away? A chasm is opened up, a resentment that cannot be filled with cheery conversation, it seemed. Even Kate was sometimes lost for words, but she came to the rescue.

'We went to a wonderful exhibition today. All kinds of models, artworks, objects. I guess you could call it modern art, but it was more than that. Pippa went crazy when she saw this giant damsel fly made from wicker, I think.'

'Mum!'

'You did. It was like looking for her when she was five, climbing inside some winding play structure.'

'I saw one of those once on a trip to Japan, in a park. I think it was a damsel fly. Could have been a grasshopper.

I can't remember now,' he added, grateful to be able to contribute something relevant.

Pippa stood up and hunkered down on the sofa with her phone, not particularly in a bad mood, but disengaged, rhythmically drawing out strands of her long hair like a semptress or a lacemaker preparing thread.

In the night, Kate was an older version of herself, taking him on top and guiding him in. Her crimped golden hair was a cape thrown over him, helping him sink into her, crawl into the cavity that was opening up in the dark.

Kate had undergone a change. She had come under the influence of a guru of sorts, a neat freak, who prided herself on the idea of tidiness, of putting everything neatly in its place. Hardly an original idea, it had to be said, but it had revivified her and their life together, given her more energy, more purpose, even improved the sex they had. Despite this, she had given up on his ever following her lead, as he had no natural ability in this area. He just wasn't practical-minded. But he did have one great quality, the capacity to be edged out of the picture, to be marginalised, and therefore, paradoxically, to be meaningful, something which fitted well with the idea of tidying up.

She continued to indulge him in his monthly massages, as expensive as they were, and she had no qualms about their always being administered by a woman, doubtless petite and pretty. He had not said it in so many words but over the years he had dropped plenty of hints, however unconsciously. And Pippa was, well, in another world, preparing for her university entrance exams now, possessed of a determination so overwhelming that everything around her seemed shut out. She would work at the kitchen table or her desk upstairs from the time she got home till past midnight, and if there were holidays, she would do the same all day, only taking the occasional rest.

At some stage, his masseuse, Lisa, showed him a picture of her own daughter, who was about thirteen at the time. That must have been about two years before. He had been genuinely surprised, because she had never spoken of a partner. The girl was a perfect image of her mother, slim, and small, scaled down as one would imagine, and in that photo they were smiling, beaming, as a perfect pair, independent of the world around. They both wore Alice bands and one-piece dresses. He had a crazy idea he would like to see them both one day, be in their company, but he had to shut it out the minute it had crossed his mind.

He did not know how long he had drifted off. It was not quite that disembodied feeling of still being massaged after it had finished, not quite that familiar, continuous wave. It was another kind of drifting, as if on water, or on a mattress while an earth tremor – or what he thought was an earth tremor – took place, the kind he was not quite sure was actually happening or might be the result of some temporary disorientation. But he heard another person in the room. How could that be the case? And then the voice did not sound quite right, younger than Pippa's, and also more light-hearted in whatever it was responding to.

He felt the oil going on. But were they Lisa's hands applying the oil? The pressure seemed lighter, the touch more tentative, the area of contact with the skin smaller. Suddenly, the familiar pressure was there again as Lisa's hands drove down on him like a luge along his calves, making furrows and displacing flesh as they went. He was happy to stay like this for a while till his mind caught up with its surroundings. As long as he was face-down, which was always how he started a massage, he would not be quite sure where he was. Even when he was directed to turn over, face-up, he did not quite know, given that his eyes were, as was the custom, covered by a cloth.

He was with Lisa, now he was sure, but not in the way he had imagined. When she took off the cloth, he saw the oval-shaped face of a girl a few years younger than Pippa, perhaps fifteen or sixteen, looking beatifically at him, and Lisa herself was looking contented but concerned. Their mutual features seemed so precise, detailed, and of a piece that he thought he could have been looking at sixteenth-century English miniatures by the same artist. When she raised the hinged head rest, his torso inclined as it always did, and he had that familiar sensation of falling into himself. But this was different. The towel that covered his lower half was lifted. He looked down at his legs. He could see them, but not feel them. A small panic started to climb up in his chest. Mercifully, sensation soon returned there. A minor case of extreme pins and needles, he told himself. He hoped his sudden startlement had not been obvious. For a brief few seconds, he had become a little dizzy and wondered if he was in a hospital being visited by friends.

'Hello,' said the girl.

'This is Rika,' Lisa said. 'We were having some fun at your expense. Rika wanted to see me at work and this is the first time she's ever been here. I hope it's O.K.'

He did not want to ask if Rika had actually touched him. He could be wrong and really offend them.

Lisa turned over and pushed her rump up, almost doubled, her vulva visible from behind. He slipped in smoothly, amazed he could actually do it easily and maintain an erection. Was it because of her small size, or just her simple acceptance of him? Although he could not see her face like this, he saw it in his mind's eye, and imagined a satisfied concentration on it, a little like he imagined her when she massaged him. No need to force it, no need to imagine that she was allowing him just to appease him. She motioned that she wanted to face him, so he eased out and brought her round. Her breasts were tiny, so tiny they were like a 2D printed image of breasts. But they lost none of their attraction for him, for that. She saw his distraction, and, vying for more, less focused attention, put her arms round his neck and pulled him down.

Rika ran at him as soon as he got in the door and launched into a worryingly energetic jump aimed at his midriff. Hardly having put his bag down, he caught the seven-year-old, holding her like a beach inflatable strapped round him. Mercifully, she was about as slightly built as her mother. Would she be the same as Lisa when she was seventeen, twenty-seven, thirty-seven?

'Daddy!'

'Yes?'

'I got the best score in class today! Isn't that great?'

'That's wonderful, baby. That's really good,' he encouraged, letting her down gently.

During supper, Rika would barely stop talking.

Lisa looked almost apologetic and seemed eager to hold him as soon as she was in bed. But then they heard Rika calling to be read to.

She sighed.

'It's OK. Won't be long.'

Upstairs, on the landing, he put on his mock-gruff voice as if donning a pantomime costume, and heard Rika giggling in response. Then, as he came into the room, he held out his hands, Frankenstein fashion, threatening to whisk her away in his rigid, frightening arms, whereupon she hid under the bedclothes.

'Little girl,' he said. 'Do not be afeared. I have to take you away for my master, a beautiful, handsome prince who lives alone in his castle.'

'Why?' she said, peeping from under the blanket.

'Because . . . he needs something sweet . . .'

'No, I mean why does he live alone in a castle?'

'My dear, he has never found a woman beautiful enough to . . .'

'But I'm too young!'

'Oh, my master will be patient. Don't worry about that.'

'But what will I do while he is waiting?'

'Why, live in the castle, of course!' he laughed. 'The castle has a magic garden where you can visit every place in the world. You just have to walk around and wish it. The time will pass quickly, believe me.'

'Ah, that sounds good.'

'So you'll let me take you away?'

She retreated under her blanket. He felt her thinking about it.

Slowly, she came out, looking him directly in the eye, as if carefully auditioning him for the role of the guardian suitable enough to take her away. Then, in a serious tone, she said, 'I have to ask Mummy what she thinks.'

'Well, it's something for you to think about tonight, isn't it?' he said, and kissed her on the forehead.

Downstairs, Rika was asleep on the sofa. The play-acting had taken longer than he had thought.

'Are you going to hers tomorrow?' she said, half-asleep. Did she know what she was saying? Would she remember tomorrow?

He was lying face-down on the table. First, they wiped his feet with a hot cloth. Then a hand applied oil and moved roughly up his right calf, the thumb kneading it and the fingers clinging to his shins, making him feel the texture of the bone there, an unpleasant feeling, really. The other sent oil lusciously up the other calf, leaving his shin alone. Next, a hand moved up the inside of his right leg, teasing out a space that really shouldn't exist, so that she did not touch his scrotum. Her actions were focused and efficient. The one on the left attacked his leg with more energy, pressing more, with less care, as she went higher and brushed his balls with the back of her hand, apparently without the intention to stimulate, faintly alerting the hairs and the chicken-skin-like lining of his testicles, the amazing part of his anatomy which he remembered as a young boy constantly moving within its fluid housing, working effortlessly to generate sperm, an activity he rarely felt happening now. He had to turn his thoughts away. They both shifted to the far sides of his legs, the first concentrating on the slight dip to the side of his pelvis, the other the more peremptory in her ministrations in this area.

The first also differed in that she massaged his buttocks without any circumspection, whereas the second went straight to his lower back and up. Every step of the way, he was coated in oil. The first continued up his back. In this area, and around the shoulders and neck there was little difference. Without speaking, they guided him to turn over onto his back, covering his eyes with a light cloth. He did not peep. The first put oil on his torso and as her hands descended down, he almost giggled as they worked their way shyly around his nipples. The second started at his feet again, going up his shins, again very smoothly, but not pressing too hard. The first was now repeating similar actions, but she was unused to doing this side of him, he now thought. The second gently worked inside his thigh now and as she did so gently pushed aside the head of his penis, which stirred slightly, the activity in his scrotum starting up like some old engine being cranked on a wheel. He was fighting it, to some extent, but it was so pleasurable, intended or not. The first was much more careful only going up the inside as far as was necessary without touching him there. On the other side, his excitement was less palpable as his penis was limply rested away from her, like a drunk on the side of the road, unlikely to be woken by anyone or anything. Yet . . .

When he felt it, he tried to sit up a little, but a hand firmly held him down. Whose it was, he could not have said, but he did not offer any real resistance as he felt his balls surrounded by the heat of a mouth, taking them in completely. As the tongue lifted one ball and the other, it was as if they had been given back their true, integral motion, threatening to orbit each other in their double casing, as they twisted like some dangling modern art masterpiece by Eva Hesse. As she let them out, a hair snagged on her teeth and that was painful for a while, but she brought up a finger to release it. The other (first?, second?), preferred to lick the outside first, letting the sac sit on her tongue like a fruit being tasted for the first time, then closing her mouth around it and drawing it down, biting lightly into the upper receding sides, a hot air balloon in reverse that went into the rest of his body. That was the first, he decided.

The second now worked the glans with her mouth enough to draw some threads of pre-semen out, a delicate gossamer he imagined forming a hammock in the air, anchored on her lip as she withdrew. The first, inevitably, compressed his shaft and let her teeth sink a little, not only biting lightly at the base but drawing her teeth carefully along back to the head, releasing and starting again at intervals as she went, partly to breathe properly and partly to reduce abrading the skin.

They drew the knife down him from his scalp, peeling back the skin perfectly. To form flaps on both sides. Wonderfully, no blood spilled anywhere, even as they took out his organs. They discussed and looked at each organ as they reached in, pulled one out, and turned it in their hands, sometimes gifting each other one that they were not so interested in, placing them in a plastic laundry basket on either side. It was strange that he could still feel these organs, as much as one could any organ inside one, even as he looked at them in their sequestered states, seeing them with his own eyes. The latter, mercifully, had been left in place, with his brain.

His stomach now a hollow pit, they had a dilemma, as they reached his manhood. How to keep it straight while dividing it? Did he have Peyronie's disease? they speculated? Well, now. There is only one way to know for sure.

One hand moved down the base, cradling it. Erect, it was dead centre, they agreed. They would have to be quick. Only one chance.

The implement was wielded perfectly. In an instant, his penis was split perfectly in two, the two halves splayed to the sides like the longitudinal peel of a banana.

Finally, they split him apart, taking one complete half each, with their favourite organs.

In the corridor, there was activity, as he was carried out and down the stairs on two separate stretchers. Outside, he was put on a trolley, the organs placed neatly underneath in proper plastic containers.

On his right, he saw Pippa, crying or smiling he couldn't say. On his left, he saw Rika, in a similarly ambiguous pose. They were in their early twenties now, it seemed.

In the street, with a huge crowd gathered around, the two were lined up next to each other, but this time the wrong way round, so that his two hands could touch, for a moment, and through the serendipity of geometry, he could see himself as complete, even as he saw himself eye to eye, twice, as if there were two of him, instead of two halves.

The Tableau

I WAKE FROM the dream. Martin is sleeping beside
me. The moon is casting a trapezoid of light across
our heads and over where our arms should be, under the
sheets. I say where they should be, because I'm not totally
certain I've actually woken from the dream. Who knows
if the dream isn't still tricking me? Who can say that our
arms haven't been lopped off and the blood isn't seeping
down into the pit of the bed? Dream or not, I can't have
screamed or made much noise because Martin is sleeping
on, oblivious. He looks like an angel. How could I have
been thinking of Alex like that?

I decide that the dream is too good not to record. I know
that if I go back to sleep, it will be lost, so I get up and go
to the study. My room is a rather lurid purple approaching
indigo, but I like it like that. There are plenty of postcards –
Picasso, Magritte, Delvaux, Balthus (oh, Balthus!), Willink,
Carrington, dear Carrington, to name a few.

Switching on the angle-poise, I quickly write up the
dream, connecting to the internet out of habit. Then, as
if recalled memory and reality have found just the right
moment to dovetail, almost like that moment in so many of

the great surrealist Belgian's paintings – I mean Magritte here – where you can't tell whether a line is the silhouette of one form in the foreground or its neighbour receding into the background, where it seems as if there is a danger of one plane slipping into another dimension, dissolving perspective, I feel a trickle between my legs and I realise, too late, some semen is starting to escape – residue of our real love making of – what is it now? – an hour and a half ago?

I rush to the bathroom and wipe myself. Soaking up the remnants of that little flood, I place a precautionary sanitary towel between knickers and that soft bed of flesh, as if my lover's hands are cupping me. Precautionary, because my period is due, though I am usually off a few days, no matter how assiduously I mark the calendar.

On my way back to bed, I hear a perky gentle drum roll from the speakers of my computer, which tells me Alex has somehow managed to stay up this late, too, and is online, keen for a chat. Normally, I would be dying for some dirty talk, but I hope he's not in the mood for that right now. I'm tired, I say to myself, but . . . what the heck.

I bring up the flashing window, which sits at the bottom of my screen flagging itself like a Boschian owl sitting patiently on a tree branch, waiting, waiting.

'How far can I put my fist in your cunt, do you think?'

This intro is par for the course. Admittedly, it's continuing from roughly where we left off last time – when Martin came home a little earlier than usual.

We have never met, Alex and I, though we've exchanged photos. He has that ridiculous drop-dead-handsome-chiselled-square-jawed-five-o'-clock-shadow face that you only see on models. Not the kind of guy you imagine needing to feed disembodied nocturnal fantasies hunched over a machine.

'Not even a "What are you doing up at this hour?"' I joke.

'Sorry, I thought that's what you would like, especially at this hour.'

'Appreciate it, but I ain't in the mood.'

'Oh.'

'But I do have something interesting to tell.'

'Yes?' This response is accompanied by a cringey smiley icon.

'I dreamt about you. At least, you were in there somewhere, looking on.'

'That figures. Was it good?'

'It wasn't exactly what you might think.'

I cut and pasted the thing to him. My empty, minimised rectangular window waited on his response, non-committal.

'That's quite odd.'

'Yes, 'tis true.'

There was another pause, the kind of pause where I knew he was straining to find just the right follow-up, but his typed words came quicker than I expected:

'My mother always said, "Saturday's dream/Sunday told/ Sure to come true/However old".'

'Is it Saturday?'

'We just crossed over. It depends how technical you want to be.'

'You do make me laugh!'

'I want you to drink my semen.'

'That's more in character. Alex . . . don't take this the wrong way . . . we made love earlier, and it seems, well, you know . . . Maybe in a few days I'll be up for it? If you can wait that long.'

'I'll make do.'

'Yes, I know you will.'

'Night night, then.'

'Night.'

Next morning when I wake up, I have a vague inkling that I dreamt something strange in the night, but I'm not quite sure. I check my files, and the dream is confirmed, and with it, the memory of the late-night dialogue with Alex. The knowledge is a relief. It was real.

As soon as Martin is out of the house, I start work. I go back up the stairs to my studio and face a new canvas. It's weeks since I finished my last painting and that dream, like some present, has been gifted to me, giving me something to hold on to. I have to think of the underlying tone of this painting now, and it's definitely brown, so I'm going to go for a warm but dull ground. While that is drying, and it will take some hours, I do a sketch. I don't have the elements all together yet, and though they will inevitably wander, and take a final, different shape, I am grateful for that last image from the dream as a starting point.

Which is the baby, I think. The idea of that helpless baby crying on the floor is powerful enough. Or is it a doll? Somehow that is even creepier. I decide to draw the baby in the form of a doll, for now.

The pane of glass that allows a view into the room-within-a-room is like a canvas placed over the whole scene, drawing attention to the scene within, *trompe-l'oeil*-fashion.

It's as if you are looking at a TV screen built into a wall and you really think there's a person there in the next room, but you're not sure.

Inside, the art historian teacher is sitting in one corner; she has short, mannish hair and narrow, black-rimmed glasses, a concentrated, searching expression on her face. She's wearing a short, tight skirt and her legs are crossed. Her red-haired daughter is standing on the opposite side, slightly closer to us, attempting to face her mother down but revealing some hesitation with her posture and slightly-parted lips. I feel there should be another figure in the office, a woman, though I don't know.

We don't have a child, Martin and I, and in fact we are agreed we don't want one. I wouldn't say I think often of kids, to be honest, if at all. It's a question of choice and freedom. I just don't give that much thought to children, which is why it's all the more surprising that one crops up in a dream like this. Maybe it's some kind of regret, now that I am nearly forty.

I work for about three hours and try to take a rest by going into the village for a drive. We live near Dartmoor, so when the ideas, the telly, and the internet are crowding out my mind too much, that's where I go, or else in the other direction to one of the seaside towns. I don't have mystical encounters, I'm not a New Age nut, but I can clear my mind out there, just about, or at least long enough for other, more useful, formed thoughts to come rushing in, which I can then run back home with, as if they are some protected species of bird I've taken from the moor.

I've been with Martin since university, and nothing can be said to be wrong with us. Just over-familiarity, perhaps.

He doesn't like travelling much. I have a longing for travel, but a certain fear of big cities. I have a number of phobias, though, that make travel an almost insurmountable obstacle. Added to big cities, I have a fear of underground trains, tunnels, lifts, bridges, high places, in fact almost anything claustrophobic or vertigo-inducing in the outside world. These phobias are not incapacitating and in some ways they have made life more manageable. In a sense, they have taken the stress out of the possibility of having to meet up with Alex. Yet occasionally I have to overcome them. And then there is Alex to consider. I don't know that much about his living environment, just that he lives in London.

I walk on the moor for a while, watch tourists circumnavigate a cluster of tors, then start to climb over them. The image of the apes gathering around the monolith in *2001: A Space Odyssey* comes to mind, but I have no epiphany.

Fear or not, I shall have to go to London. I just need the right occasion for it. I hate going to London, but I simply have to, from time to time.

I can't face the canvas when I get back, but that's fine; I work as the mood takes me.

When I go online, Alex is already there, again, and I submit, willingly, to his persistence.

'Hi!' he types, eagerly.

'Hi.'

'Has it been a creative day?' I'm never quite sure if comments like these aren't edged with a little irony.

'Now you ask, yes, actually.'

'You did some painting?'

'Started something, yes.'

'I'd like to see it.'

'It's a bit derivative.'

'I'm sure you're just being modest. Have you been thinking about me?'

'A little. Actually . . . I was thinking that I might come up to London.'

'Really? Will we finally meet?'

'There's a good chance.'

'When are you thinking of?'

'Next week some time. Any time would be O.K., really, but I want to check with the gallery when's best.'

'I was thinking about you, anyway.'

'How exactly?'

'I was whipping you.'

'Really?'

'I was whipping your breasts. And your cunt.'

'Nice.'

'Aiming for your nipples.'

'Good.'

'Then I used a cane, on the inside of your thighs, gently at first.'

'Even better.'

'I thought you would like that.'

'Yes.'

'Can it possibly be as good as this when we meet? Won't one of us, at least, be disappointed?'

'No, I don't think so,' I say.

'I like it that you're so positive.'

'I like these fantasies. They give me ideas.'

'But you're not afraid of the reality?'

'No. I know you, after all this time.'

'Good.'

We chat a while longer, until Martin comes home.

'I'd better go. I'll let you know when. See you.'

'See you.'

Well, I think. I do have one person I can always see in London. My mother.

The Gallery is near Sloane Square. I take two smaller canvases up with me, along with various slides. Petra, a neat, power-dressing Austrian woman in her mid-thirties, I estimate, speaks as if she has corralled the peculiarities of English to her satisfaction and regimented their usage accordingly; her enunciation is clipped, controlled, almost scary. Something about her always made me see Otto Dix's *Portrait of the Journalist Sylvia von Harden*, albeit Petra is a good deal more feminine.

'Can I hold on to them for a few days? I want to show them to my partner, if that is O.K.? Are you up for long?'

'Yes, yes, and for a few days, actually,' seems to be the best way to answer the log jam of questions.

We take a walk around the gallery's current exhibition, an 'installation'.

At first, I think, *Oh, no, not another one of those pretentious things. People who can't paint, who just have IDEAS,* but this one is different. It features several artists who have been asked to produce one work each on seemingly unrelated topics.

I like the variety of works, for once. One is a collage of found objects, another a huge photographic light box, another a fairly traditional sculpture, yet another a well-known film playing in incredibly slow motion, another a more traditional 'experimental' film by comparison, another a painting in *ukiyo-e* style, then an exquisite oil painting (a nude), after that a larger space that looks like a jumble sale specifically put on for the benefit of theatrical and film costume designers and . . . a copper-haired woman standing in a glass case. I don't know how long she is able to stand there like that, but I reason that it's not so very different to what a model has to do sometimes. There are other displays, but these stand out most.

'Some of the installations or works are changed after a few days, to maximise the number of artists and space, you know.' Petra's sentences are a tense roller-coaster-ride, her intonation flowing up to high peaks of Germanic self-confidence and down into baritone troughs of sternness.

'It's fantastic. I'm impressed. Who's responsible for the overall concept?'

'My partner. We wanted to invite certain artists and see if their ideas would somehow form a whole vision, but at the moment I am not so sure.'

'There's something common to them all, I feel, a uniting vision, but it's as if there are one or two pieces missing,' I offer, tentatively.

'Thank you for your assessment. Perhaps by the end it will have come together, but so far it has proved popular. It is a pity we did not know of your work earlier.'

'Thank you, too, but mine's dull compared to this.'

Then I think of my latest painting, and the dream.

'I'd like to come back and have another look. Normally, I try to keep a distance from others' work when I'm in the middle of something myself.'

'Well, any time, but actually, I thought, if you are free tonight, you might like to meet my partner?'

'I'd love to.'

'Let us meet here, then.'

Despite the fact that we haven't seen each other in six months, my mother only has time to see me in her lunch break around the corner from the university where she teaches.

'How's the painting going?'

'Just started something.

You might like it for once.'

'Oh?'

'It's quite surreal; not my usual stuff. From deep in the psyche, I think.'

'How so?'

'At the moment it's based on a dream I had. But it's more like a scene out of Balthus or Delvaux . . . or Magritte. Dix, at a push.'

'Well, I'd love to see it some time.'

'Really?'

'Yes, really.'

'Well, if Petra likes it, she may find a place for it in her new installation, with any luck,' I stated with untypical confidence.

'Well, marvellous.'

'I think it might be about you and me, indirectly.'

'Do you think it's wise to talk about a work in progress, darling?'

'Maybe not, but I feel differently about this one.'

'Do you remember all those times you refused to let me

see what you were working on, even at college?'

'You of all people can understand the reason for that, surely?'

'What? Because I teach, I'm supposed to know everything that goes on in an artist's mind?'

'Well, it's not just any artist, is it?'

'Is this really what you want to talk to me about?

'No. I want to talk about the dream.'

'I'm hardly a psychologist, darling.'

'Let me just tell you. It won't take long. Take a deep breath,' I started in, expecting her eyes to glaze over almost immediately. 'It's like this.

'It's late, you see, and I'm in a dark street, you know the kind, that looks like something out of *The Third Man* or one of Nabokov's Berlin streets, and I stumble across Alex . . .'

'Alex?'

'It's just a name,' I explained, hoping she wouldn't press me.

'He's working as an undercover policeman. He sees me and tells me politely to get out of the area. I go down a side street saying to myself, *Now that's a man, that is.* Are you listening?'

'Yes, dear, I'm listening. It's positively riveting . . .'

'Anyway, I feel an overwhelming warmth for him, this man. Then I'm lost, and I ask someone, maybe a newspaper-seller in a cloth cap, I'm not quite sure, for directions. He shows me up some stairs to an old tube station. We get in a lift, which seems to move forward on very narrow tracks like a tiny tube train, so that you can see the twists and turns as it goes through the tunnel, like a mobile concertina. It reaches a building and lets me out, like any normal lift would, onto the first floor of a building; I see a young woman with flame-red hair who reminds me of the art historian teacher I am visiting.'

'Art historian!' my mother exclaims.

'It's her daughter, I realise (my mother just about suppresses a semaphore of indignation). I follow her until I reach the art historian's office, into which I can see through a large plate glass window. It's a bit like one of those poky cubicle-cum-offices that you get in telephone canvassing companies or language schools. Anyway, inside I see some kind of *tableau vivant* (although I don't know it at first). There's a baby under a table and one of the inexplicable casters under the table leg is being moved repeatedly over the crying baby's hand. I burst in and shout something to the effect that they have to stop because the baby is being hurt, but I'm told it's some kind of staged event. They just laugh at me.'

My mother had seemed pretty aloof during all this, as I had expected, until I got to the part about the baby on the floor, in the office, and I was wondering if there wasn't a tear beginning to form in the corner her eye.

'Is something wrong?'

'No, no, I think something got in my eye, that's all,' she said, dabbing at what I was sure now must be tears.

'Do you think it means anything?'

'I hope you don't want to say it's a premonition, darling.'

'It doesn't have to be about something that's going to happen, surely?'

'No, I suppose not.'

'Any ideas? Can you interpret it like you would a paint-ing?' I pushed.

'It seems obvious, don't you think? If this young woman with red hair is following her mother, or looking at her or just listening to her – it's hard to tell – who's an art historian . . .'

'You think the red-headed girl is me? Then who is following the daughter? Who is watching all this?'

'Well, you can stand outside yourself, can't you? Especially in a dream.'

'Yes, I suppose so, mother.'

'And then there's this baby being hurt and me wanting to stop it. What could that be?'

'I really can't imagine. It *is* just a dream. Can't a dream just be a dream?'

'Maybe, maybe,' I say, finally backing down, realising I've left out the bit about feeling I am being watched too, maybe by Alex.

I decide to stop because I sense she is becoming edgy. It's obvious I've touched a nerve in her, though I can never be certain, with my mother. When she wants to dissemble, she's a past mistress.

I meet Alex in a wine bar in the West End.

I'm thinking he will be disappointed when I tell him I'm busy tonight, but there's still time for a potential meeting later.

'It *is* Alex, isn't it?' I say a little, dizzily. I try to affect confidence and authority on these kinds of occasions but often as not I come across as a lost little girl, like a miniaturised Ally McBeal scuttling away behind the office desk.

'Dara?' It's not so much his voice that answers as his angled jaw, I decide. I'm speaking to a human part, a part of a whole, I think, but a part nonetheless. *Will he turn out to be human at all?* I speculate, very idly.

'It's strange, isn't it?' I say. 'After all this time?'

'Yes.'

I suddenly think, *This is not going to work.* We're never going to be able to talk the way we talk on chat, not like this. We need something to focus on. Then it occurs to me. I would feel much safer if I were to take Alex with me to Petra's.

He agrees.

In the hour and a half that follows, he doesn't really let on much about himself. I had half expected this. But I tell him about myself. I hardly stop talking for the best part of an hour, my monologue punctuated only by time taken out to order food and drink. While I'm speaking, lurid visions nudge themselves into consciousness – clichéd images of how he must live and . . . *live out* his fantasies. He has some kind of mock dungeon in the cellar with an array of bondage gear and instruments, masks, whips, chains, riding crops, breast talons, nipple clamps, pliers, hammers, an iron maiden, miscellaneous torture instruments that deploy a complex system of pulleys and levers, power drills . . .

'Don't you think,' I put in at one point, 'that with the internet, people are actually doing less of this sort of thing, the whole BDSM scene?'

'I hadn't. Why?'

'Well, my theory is that because it's so accessible nowadays, more people can live out their fantasies at a remove,' I reason.

'What about you, though? Do you want to live it

vicariously, or do you want to go through it yourself?'

I don't answer, I can't. There is no obvious reason for my interest in this area – if you forget the impressions made on me at an early age by such tomes as *The Story of O* and *Justine*.

'Anyway, how many of these people are in it for real?' he says defensively. 'Where do they get the time to build and buy all these materials, to have endless access to willing partners in the first place?'

He seems to rethink his words.

'My vision of horror is to be trapped in some Home Counties cellar with someone who really means it, to be held captive by some Fred and Rose West in Sevenoaks, let alone in Gloucester.'

He pauses a while.

'Don't worry. I won't be inviting you back to my pad.' On the internet I might have expected a reassuring smiley here, a grin, even, but in real life there is nothing. Not the real thing itself.

Then it dawns on me: he's married. *Oh, fuck it, Dara.*

'In that case, let's go and take in some *kultcha*,' I quip, despite my sudden misgiving.

'Yes, let's.'

It is in the taxi, which Alex offered to pay for, that I start to feel drowsy. I remember Alex's hand starting to go round my shoulder, then I am in the grip of what I can only describe as a waking dream. I am still in the taxi, but I feel as if we are in an underground train burrowing under London, like a giant worm, bunching itself up in segments, then expanding. We are both in a long vehicle and in a short one at the same time, and I feel as if I am suffocating every time we round a bend.

We come to a lift and I am helped or pushed, I don't know which, inside. We come out into a spacious room full of *objets d'art* and paintings. We stand there a while. A red-haired woman comes along to help Alex take off my clothes, though I am still standing. She walks off with them, and I follow her instinctively, as if I can get them back. But the atmosphere is more consistent with a film by Pasolini than it is with Borowczyk, to my chagrin.

I walk behind her until she reaches a room, almost a cubicle, separated from the main one only by a partition, which from waist height upwards is all plate glass. Inside the room, on a sofa, in profile, sits Petra. On another chair in the corner sits my mother, like a wax dummy. Behind me, on the table by the glass partition, Alex is making love to the redhead, and every time the table, which is on casters, moves, it runs over the hand of a small baby which is also a doll and which cries out every time.

I stand in front of Petra and she starts talking incessantly about the painting that hangs over the sofa.

Alex and the young woman suddenly stop and turn to us. They push me onto Petra, groping me all the while, inserting their fingers in my arse, my cunt, my mouth, every bloody damned orifice. Petra does not move as they push me on her. She just keeps on talking about art, art, art. She is the ground, she says, the layer, for the painting. I feel her body becoming mollescent, on the way to liquid. Alex's stringy, glutinous semen arcs over us, incessantly; the redhead's saliva, her urine, her vaginal juices impregnate our merging skins. My mother, her body rigor mortis stiff, still sits in the corner, pointedly, but she is speaking now.

First, I hear, 'Do you think it's wise to talk about a work in progress, darling?'

Then, 'I really can't imagine. It *is* just a dream. Can't a dream just be a dream?'

All this time, I feel myself flattening, softening, then hardening; my limbs are pushed to the four extremities, up against the wall above the sofa. I am made of wood, plaster, brick, bone, flesh, paint. I am all over.

Finally, I am standing outside this scene again, looking in at the room behind the glass with its tableau of occupants: my mother in the corner, Petra now back on the sofa, with Alex and the copperhead on the table making love and looking on at Petra, as she lectures on the canvas on the wall. That painting, above the sofa, shows the scene inside the room in which its occupants now stand in like manner: the baby with its hand being run over by the casters on the table as Alex and the woman rock back and forth, my mother in the chair, and Petra in front of the canvas lecturing on the canvas in front of her showing Alex and the woman on the table . . . seemingly forever.

Meeting Julie Christie

COINCIDENCE CAN BE a deceptive thing, sewing signif-
icance into the cloth of lives otherwise bare of all but
the most incidental interest. It can also operate on different
scales. We might be talking about two simultaneous events
that question logic or about a series of rhymes that punc-
tuate a life. Sometimes it does seem to carry meaning to
mutual agreement, sometimes the fact of it falls as flat as a
joke at a wake. I shall refrain from drawing any conclusions.
I offer only the framework.

As an active teenager I had few worries, a clan of bellig-
erent neighbours apart. Though they caused me and my
parents much harm, they were gone within the space of two
or three years. So what I still remember is on the one hand
the playing in the streets, the go-karting, and the battles
royal atop rickety fences, and on the other hand the long
climb towards academia via a boy's school, and no girlfriend
for most of that time. Whether I was not equipped with
the natural gift for attracting girls at that time, or I just
accepted the unnecessity of it, the fact is that around the
age of eleven I entered a tunnel of self-imposed learning
and hard work I did not emerge from till I was sixteen.

My best friend seemed to inhabit similar territory for most of the same period. Our longings (whatever they were) were sublimated into collecting T.Rex singles, going on guerilla missions to newsagents to increase our mutual collections of men's magazines, and polite, restrained tennis matches in the local park where the only sweet spot was to be espied in the vanishing point of a gently dipping cleavage. And at this time we are talking about when for me a trip out of my neighbourhood was intrepid, bounded as it was by a triangle of bullies who seemed to be in radio contact to prevent me from discovering more of the world.

Perhaps my affinity with Mark was only the enforced one of childhood, of a kind of superficial friendship, because it did not outlive its first real blow. That blow came in the enticingly disguised form of glamour, a glamorous coincidence that perhaps foreshadowed a dawning jealousy.

He turned up one day on his Choppa and excitedly told me he had met Julie Christie. She had come to his front door asking questions; she was taking part in some survey or other. I am quite gullible and I saw no reason to disbelieve him. I still see no reason to think otherwise. What I saw was simply an enormous injustice. What *I* would have said, what *I* would have done at that moment!

I open my front door.

'Hello, I'm Julie Christie. I'm taking part in a survey. Can I just ask you a few questions?'

Miraculously, my parents are not at home. It's summer. My Dad's working and my Mum's shopping. In the flush of youth, I have no thought of feeling embarrassed about our humble south London council house. She comes in and accepts a tea. Is she aware, is she thinking now, of how many times I've sat and watched that film set in Venice, watched *that* scene near the beginning, with my parents, all of us, in dreamy awe, in languorous excitement. Does she know that I'm going to be fascinated for the rest of my life by the idea of restoring art, of candlelit churches, and falling scaffolding? Am I not a little tempted to trip and spill the tea so that I fall into her arms, and as the liquid is slowly, indifferently absorbed by our browning carpet, she cradles me until we subside into what we have known was coming for so long? That would have been my scenario. Mark's was more mundane. 'You missed your chance,' I said to antagonise. 'What d'you mean?' he returned. I am not a good quipper. 'I don't know,' I said. 'I don't know.' Shortly after that episode Mark found his first girlfriend. They later married and they're still together now.

So I find myself walking along the South Bank, having just inspected the serried lines of Penguins and other paperbacks displayed on the stalls outside the National Film Theatre Restaurant under Waterloo Bridge. I can never put from my mind the thought that the books are doing more than just being there. They are there for *me*. I know that my decision to go and browse there is almost astrologically calculated to coincide with the placing of some addition that might change my life irrevocably. Or at least so I would like it to be. I sometimes wonder if book-buying in a sickness. I know that there are enough new books around to tie up my free hours for the rest of my life, but still there is the compulsion to scan the covers, to flick the flyleaves, to riffle through those darkening pages.

Somehow I manage to resist three or four books I haven't seen there before, and enter the café in a somewhat miserable state of mind. The place is a refuge, possessing the impersonality of a haven for private passions where people not past their earliest fascinations commingle in a mute dance of alleviation and embarrassment.

I am twenty-six now, and, unbelievably, a virgin. Not on principle, just through bad luck. I just don't have the swagger to pull myself into a relationship, to pull myself into life, you might say. Yet I'm not defeatist, either. I've brought many a girl along here, passed pleasant evenings, held hands as nondescript boats have made their way sluggishly and anonymously towards Hungerford Bridge. Our paths have often crossed those of the rival music lovers coming out of the Royal Festival Hall, too, and I've suddenly been overcome by the sense that I'm not participating sufficiently in my life. I've contemplated too long the insistent nakedness under their clothes of English girls in summer, an insistence that denies.

I work in the nearby Shell building, and I like it; it's executive heaven, and sometimes I almost feel guilty. Yet I'm failing. Don't ask me why, for God's sake; just let me indulge my passion – the benches on the South Bank, the books, the gloomy bridges like ramps to some horribly distant yet unavoidable destination in the sky.

These usual thoughts are going through my head on this particular afternoon when I become aware of a woman sitting diagonally opposite me. I resist looking up to assess in the usual manner, letting a kind of idealised image take form, from the palette of the eye's canthus. Invariably, one is shocked on these occasions to see the reality, perhaps because the intimations of line have to proceed through so many intermediaries, of experience, of fantasy, of tension, quite apart from the sheer optical limitations.

I am shocked, but for a different reason.

I am looking at Julie Christie, sitting almost opposite me, calmly writing away, completely unfazed by my astonishment. I wonder, and look around. No one else is gawping, making me wonder whether I'm mistaken.

I look again. I'm not mistaken. I think to myself that normally one wouldn't have a starting point in a situation like this. But I have that niggling childhood memory, that little anecdote that could see me into the first lap of conversation with her. But no, it's not enough. I don't want to be some film bore; I'm no critic. And she certainly won't remember my friend from fifteen years back. She writes on, oblivious. Incredibly, I'm the first to leave. I can't even bear to look back.

No one told me I had reason to be hopeful in life.

My wife is sitting on the other side of the train compartment. She has a way of looking at me that I've never seen in anyone else, a kind of worrying away at her features that in any other person would be a dirty look but which in her is more an invitation to some pleasant conspiracy.

We're on our honeymoon, Venice, the kind of place you go to at this stage in life (I'm thirty-five now) not expecting anything too extraordinary from since you've seen it on TV, in films, and read about it in books so often that it seems almost perverse actually to be engaged by it. In fact, there are two ways you can react. You can have the clichéd image reinforced, you can insist on it as your right, or you can let the image before your eyes seep slowly into the one you already had in your head, as if the canvas has not yet dried, so that the place before you is more than ever your place.

As yet, I am uncertain as to which way I will swing. When we stand on San Marco Square, with the crowd's behaviour almost indistinguishable from the pigeons', as they peck away at the historic sites, shitting on them with their negligent chattering, I feel Giulia's presence to be more essential than ever before.

She surprises me in this way, as she says she has never been in Venice before, but she puts it down to her training in architecture. She tells me about Alberti and Brunelleschi, and I nod to explanations of absent perspective, happy to be caught in web-like trapezoids of dawning comprehension.

As you have probably guessed, the city is to be the venue of our mutual defloration.

In a trattoria I ask her for the hundredth time what it is she sees in me, genuinely unable to comprehend. 'Everything,' she says, 'so much.' We know what to expect from each other, we are each other's rehearsal for life, for a new beginning.

We take the vaporetto on an extended and indulgent diversion to our hotel, the sun retreating in accordance with the whole show. A boy on the quay immediately before a modern block of flats belly-flops carelessly in the wake of our boat, and I think that perhaps he is a version of me, growing up in a watery south London.

Stepping off the vaporetto, we walk down forever-receding alleyways. We gain an almost unheard-of advantage over our fellow Venice trippers; an old woman agrees to let a room in her house for the week.

We have been together long enough now for words to be unnecessary. When she lets me undress her, I can't prevent the sound of a pleasing moan coming from my throat. She smiles benevolently. Her net stockings, which impose a grid of multiplying openings on finite flesh, also catch the contours of full hips and thighs, leaving me to believe I have really caught some magnificent sea creature. I am happier than ever before. We move over one another, making pleasant spiralling motions with our hands on each other's backs.

Images flash through my mind, all these images of women, those places I've been to many times alone. I regret the bitterness and resent the chances that were not given. But there has always been one constant, a pleasing shadow, watching over me. The convergence is complete, and perhaps now I can rest. I can start living at last.

The Mannikin

M Y FATHER HAD sent me the life-size mannikin with the noblest intentions in mind, to enable me to further my drawing skills and help defray any starting costs I might incur on my arrival in England. I had used many such models to guide my hand and eye till now, but this I had never seen before in the family home, and I almost feared that my father had spent too much on this construction. I say construction, but at the same time I feel almost guilty as it sits slightly folded in on itself, like a decrepit old man or woman, with its carved eyes cast down as if at something it has spied in front of it, its newly burnished wood belying its sad posture. I saw 'it' as a 'she', though I was certain that it could be adapted to give the appearance of either sex.

I left her to herself while I started to write a letter of gratitude to my father in my bare lodgings. My most recent abode had been Amsterdam, and I missed the comforting reflections of the canals visible from our home there, albeit now I was not far from the Thames, a huge, cold, sludgy river that filled me with a sense of dread; I felt its anguilliform massiveness moving into the few sleeping hours I had spent in this new country since my arrival a few weeks before. I tried to divert these sombre thoughts with those of my sweet sister Gesina, for whom I had many expectations. I had seen already in her blossoming a talent for drawing which I feared our age might stifle on account of her being a woman. I resolved to aid her in her ambitions as best I could, and it was after this optimistic contemplation that I must have fallen asleep.

I awoke to a glint of something shining in my eye. To eclipse that unwanted reflection, I moved my head only slightly and saw it was the sun deflecting from the metal goblet from which I had drunk the previous evening. Very soon, I heard movement downstairs from my uncle's workroom. Doubtless, apprentice boys were arriving, deliveries were being made, and the servants were starting about their tasks. The thoroughfare in front of my uncle's house was roughly cobbled, and I still had not quite become used to the crash of the cartwheels in the ruts between them.

My first thought after I had eaten was to finish the reply to my father's letter. I re-read what little I had put down the previous evening:

Dear Father

I have arrived safely and been welcomed by Uncle Voerst. I am now lodged in bare but nevertheless commodious circumstances. The workroom and the house are somewhat loud, to my ears, and active all week long, but I can study in peace when not called upon to be guided by Uncle's trusted hand to paint or to assist him in some way. I have enough time given to me to wander outdoors and contemplate life, despite some rancid smells in the streets, yet I would not do this at night unless accompanied.

Pausing, I looked once more at the mannikin, almost as if for permission, and I continued:

I thank you most deeply from my heart for the manni-kin and the clothes you have sent me. I understand your ambition for me in using it to the best of my abilities and to paint in the modern way. I have been told that such a model is not very common in this country. Now my thoughts turn to dressing it in a suitable fashion.

I have yet to visit His Majesty's Court, and I tremble at the thought that I might be confronted one day with the presence of his great painter, Van Dyck, and how I might greet him and praise him adequately. There is rumour that he might even one day visit Uncle's workshop.

I pray that Gesina does not miss me too much and that she is diligent with her studies.

There I stopped as I heard a knock at the door. The maid was bringing a message for me to start work downstairs. Before I left the room, I turned as if in regret that I was leaving behind the crisp Dutch light filtered through lozenge-shaped mullioned windows, but my room merely had large panes that flooded the room with dull English light. And there was something else. The mannikin. I had left it, uncovered, in the corner. I must attend to the poor thing on my return. First and foremost, it needed a stand.

'Have you eaten, my lad?' were my uncle's first words.

'No, I . . .'

'Then eat you shall. For today's work you will need energy.'

As we ate, my uncle explained:

'Today you shall mix colours. Until now you have worked little with paint?'

'Yes, sir, mainly drawings.'

'They are essential, of course, in every instance. Maybe you will yet make engravings like your uncle,' he smiled toothily. 'But today I have something very special for you. We could say that it is a project that I have, and you will learn much about paint in the process!'

Once downstairs, I was confronted with a sight I did not expect. A young woman seemingly of noble birth, was standing by the main window of the painting room. I saw her first only in profile. When she turned, the pleats in her red skirt spun like a whirly-gig, and my eye travelled up from her yellow stomacher to her lace-covered, square neck-line. My uncle introduced me just as our eyes met for the first time.

At first, I was overwhelmed, not because of her beauty, because she did indeed possess a great handsomeness of face, but because I thought I was looking at an older version of my young sister. My eye fell again quickly to her satin dress, which was of such brilliance that I was worried for my eyesight. I could say nothing for a moment.

'Well,' my uncle almost bellowed. His raised voice by itself warned me that this woman was of importance, because I already knew this not to be his normal way.

'I am truly honoured, my lady,' I said in French, kissing her hand.

'My boy, you will draw the standing figure of the lady. I leave it to you for the time being to have her take part in some . . . decorous action, such as writing a letter, receiving a visitor, whatever comes to mind, as long as she is standing. But see to it that my lady does not become too tired. Let her sit, between times.'

'Sir,' she spoke, for the first time. 'It is my honour to be the guest of such illustrious painters.'

'Hardly illustrious, my lady,' Van Voerst bowed in deference, without obsequiousness, which appealed to me, then said abruptly to me, 'Here is some chalk to start you off. You will need no more right now.'

With him gone, I asked her to walk around the room in various poses, finally deciding to have her hold a letter.

I knew to concentrate on the outlines first.

I could not presume anything of her status for sure. She might be a lowly wretch from the street dressed up for my uncle's purposes, or she might be of high birth, albeit everything in her demeanour, stance, and my uncle's form of address to her did indicate the higher rank.

I drew the outlines of a position I was satisfied with, thinking I would concentrate on her face later. I could use the mannikin for her body, and eventually another model when she was not available.

'My lady . . .'

'Yes?'

'Might I ask if . . . your dress, or something similar, could be left here at a later time, to ease the burden of your standing here too long?'

'My dress? Oh, I see. That will be taken care of . . . But tell me first how long I should be available for you.'

'One hour a day, when it pleases you. I do not know what my uncle . . .'

I could not tell from her accent where she was from, but I did not mind to guess for a while or wait till my uncle told me more. It was not long before he came back to see my efforts. He looked pleased. I would tell him later about our arrangement.

My uncle had not told me how much I should earn from a portrait, should it turn out to be a commission, but I still had much to learn in that field.

I spent a good part of the rest of that day having one of the boys build a stand for the mannikin, which I took downstairs, drawing many curious looks during the day.

To my surprise, before dusk, the lady's clothes arrived, and I set about arranging them on the figure as soon as I had a chance. With only candlelight now, I was a little overcome with an unusual anxiety, believing more and more that I had to finish this preparation quickly.

I decided to take the mannikin with its stand back up to my room.

Placing her in the corner of the room opposite the foot of my bed, it occurred to me now that I should set her at such an angle that she would catch the morning light. Haphazardly, for now, I set the bodice, stomacher, skirt, and wig on the faceless mannikin, unable in such low light to assess my efforts properly any more that night.

◊

I saw her again in the night, but it was through a misted screen. I saw my hand reaching to touch it in places as if to press through, but she moved back, unaware that the touch was mine.

'What are you?' I heard myself ask.

Her eyes were searching, as if she had heard my words, and her mouth moved, but even in this dream I heard nothing. Then, the sound came, and I heard: 'I am life, sir'. She turned, in a whirl, disappearing into the dark.

Over breakfast in the morning, I felt I should ask my uncle about his ideas.

'Sir, if I might ask you something?'

'Go ahead, young man.'

'What is better? To paint from the mind or from life, *naar 't leven*, as we say.'

'My boy, you will do well to see as many examples of drawings and paintings by the masters before you think of painting from life.'

'Indeed,' I concurred. 'Yet . . .'

'Yes?'

'Why do we use models?'

'Like the pretty lady you have been honoured to paint?' he said with a smile.

'Well, yes.'

'We have an idea in our minds, from study, do we not? We have an idea of what a good or noble person might be. We want those ideas to come before the people we see so that they might reflect in their lives the noble virtues for which we strive.'

'I see. So the person himself is merely a physical model for an idea?'

'If you wish to put it like that.'

I wanted to say further that a real person might position herself between one's ideal and the space she inhabited in nature, and ask further whether the two met at any point, but I did not want to be too forward at this early stage.

'Now, when you have done the basic outlines, I will show you a technique. You may know of it already.'

'I would need a little longer. Perhaps one more visit? She comes tomorrow.'

'That is fine.'

Upon entering my room, I decided, on seeing the light fall on the yellow bodice as it did, to leave her in place, standing at the window; I made a note of the time. To hell with what they thought downstairs, I cursed. I brought up the most essential tools and paints I needed, albeit the easel was not easy to carry up the narrow stairs. After lunch, I continued to sketch all day, falling in and out of sleep, the warp and weft of the bodice frustrating me more and more.

In the late afternoon, my uncle came up to observe what I had done. His footfall was light, like my father's, but the stairs still gave him away.

'Yes, yes,' he said, without commenting more.

'Bring that down and we shall teach you something.'

I felt a little aggrieved to have to move her once more, but there was nothing else for it, in my circumstances.

In the painting room, as light was fading, my uncle placed on an oiled canvas a sheet which had on its further side some pigment such that that side completely met and covered the canvas as a window fitting into its frame. He instructed me then to place my drawing on the unpainted side of this in-between layer and showed me how to follow the outlines in such a way as to transfer the basic lines of my drawing onto the canvas through this intermediate sheet, as it were.

An assistant peeled back the sheets.

I was pleased with the result.

'Excellent,' said my uncle. 'When does she come next?'

'Tomorrow, I believe.'

'You can start on her face.'

'I would . . . like to practise painting the material more . . . in my room.'

'I do not see why not, if you prefer.'

As I started upstairs, he said 'You feel you . . .', then stopped.

'I'm sorry, uncle?'

'Oh, no matter. Go on.'

Later, in my room, I turned again to my letter, which still was not finished. I picked up my pen:

My uncle showed me the tracing technique today. I had not the heart to let him know that you had already shown me, but the practice is not wasted. I confess that I am not happy always with this method. I would rather sketch straight to the canvas, yet perhaps I may profit from it for rendering certain materials and their sheen. As you know, satin moves at the slightest breath of the model such that there is really no other way to fix the reflections of light on such delicate material. This way, and using the manni-kin, I am assured, I might decide on the exact reflections beforehand, independently of the wearer's movements, and perhaps use the drawing again. I . . . confess to wanting more and more to be alone with the doll to work at my own speed. That is not wrong, I hope? Yet I do look forward to seeing the young lady on her return tomorrow, an event that will have long passed by the time you receive this modest description.

It was dark very soon, and the smells from the street dissuaded me once more of my idea to go out even for a brief stroll. I found also the shouts from the street and what I believed to be coarse words very unedifying. Therefore, I set to experimenting with the mannikin, to moving its limbs in all manner of ways that would conform to different postures. I generally thought that it was convenient to not have to worry about the kind of things that one would ask of a real person, to move an arm or even a leg in such a way that one could not conceive of doing with a live model. Yet, sometimes, having moved her to a chair now, I might put a limb in such a way as she sat there that I might hear a sound which seemed not exactly human but also not truly inanimate, a sound as of air being pressed or released. This would be mixed in with the sound of the rubbing of polished wood moving in a socket of some kind. I had not investigated the inner workings of this doll yet, and in truth I preferred to leave some mystery. And I certainly did not want to take apart this . . . device. I believe I was only interrupted the once, by the maid bringing me a very large glass of ale; when she saw me kneeling at the doll, she quickly withdrew, giggling.

I confess it was not wisest to investigate the creature in the dimming light and with candles, so I fell asleep till the next morning.

Yet when I awoke it was not to see the doll in the chair as I had left her, but to see her on my bed next to me, her skirt uncouthly lifted, face down. I could not recall how she had come to be in this position and quickly I lifted her up by the waist and carried her to the chair, where her head sank down as if in a sulk, reminding me of the first day when I had placed her on the floor. I examined the skirt particularly closely, worried it may have been damaged, but I was relieved to find nothing amiss.

The next day the lady was due, but she did not come. I informed my uncle of this after a half-hour had passed, and he sent a messenger out to see what was amiss.

'Uncle, I will go to look for her, if you do not mind.'

'Gerard, it is not necessary,' he almost scolded me.

'I insist . . . with respect.'

'Then take the boy.' He will see you do not get into trouble. Besides, he can speak a little Dutch, too. He has the address.'

'Oh?'

The suggestion was too sensible to refuse. The boy was a young man with red hair who did house chores and mixed pigments. I did not know if he had ambitions to paint.

We stepped out at just before the busiest time of day. I was saved almost immediately by the boy's hand from slipping on something that had spilled over from the kennel, perhaps animal guts, some tubular workings of the insides of some creature I did not care to think of.

'Careful, sir. The scavengers have not been here today yet.'

'The scavengers?'

'The men who collect the waste, sir.'

Barely had we gone more than a few streets than we were presented with the sight of a man standing relieving himself onto a small mound of waste that had built up against the side of someone's wall. I felt already like returning to my uncle's house. Perhaps the lady had arrived in the meantime?

'Is it far?'

'Perhaps a half hour, sir. Perhaps more.'

'One might hope we might see her on the way, I suppose,' I said, almost wistfully.

'Would she not come by carriage, sir?'

He was not being cheeky, this boy. I saw his concern and that he scanned the streets hard, if not a little warily, sometimes.

On the way, I did see some sights that I still remember to this day. Workmen of many trades and hues, carrying equipment of all kinds; a crier; a cleric; those who looked like they worked in workshops; a few pretty girls, but in rather bedraggled clothes; a man with no nose; a number of crones with arched backs; and, perhaps most surprisingly, a very old couple who were dressed very finely, even though I could see looking down that the woman's dress was soiled with mud and probably shit at the very bottom. She seemed unaware of this, or cared no longer. The couple both wore a strange grin.

To top this pretty picture and add to my mood, a horse sprayed filthy water over my breeches as we turned a corner. I prayed inwardly that we would arrive at a more commodious part of town before too long, and that we did, as we passed the Inns of Court and came to the Strand. There was still great activity and much din, yet the streets were altogether cleaner and the people more fashionable.

Now, the boy took me down a steep alley in the direction of The Thames. We did not go all the way down, but I saw, in a narrow corridor of view, that activity picked up greatly in this area, with many barges and skiffs on the river. On top of that, I saw many well-dressed ladies and gentlemen about to alight from their craft, doubtless at one of the water-stairs leading up to one of the great houses on the north bank of the Thames, of which I had heard so much.

As we descended further, I was regretting not having put on sturdier footwear and had already decided to take a water boat on the way home.

'This lady,' I asked the boy finally, 'is she of noble birth?'

'Indeed, sir. You will soon see.'

The boy now led me through a door in front of which there was much movement and shouting.

We emerged into one of those Italian gardens which the English were so fond of at that time and to which a number of men and women now busily attended, and I was afforded a very privileged view of a wider aspect of the Thames.

Before we were allowed to enter the house itself, the boy turned to me and said, 'Please wait here.'

I saw him walk straight up and, as he entered, I thought I espied the young lady from a window on the second floor.

It did not take long until he came out, seemingly in a hurry, saying,

'Sir, we must hurry.'

'But . . .'

'I have something . . .' he said under his breath.

I followed him out, feeling quite silly, nodding to the steward of the house as we exited.

We walked along for a while, then the boy handed me a letter folded into a tiny space.

'She said to not open it until we are returned. It is letterlocked.'

'Letterlocked?'

'Sir, let us be off, if you do not mind.'

I could endure this no longer and asked the boy to signal for a carriage to stop.

Once we were arrived, I was in no mood to explain to my curious uncle all that had happened and went straight to my room to read the letter in private. However, I first had to peel back a number of pages that had been folded over each other, held in place only by strips of paper cord tied through small holes. I read:

My dear Sir

With a heavy heart, I write in this fashion to let you know that I cannot come again. Please be aware that it has nothing to do with your own conduct or bearing towards me in any way. My circumstances have changed since your uncle was so kind as to suggest a possible portrait. For your inconvenience and recompense, I gift you the dresses which I had sent forward after our first meeting until a time when I am disposed to collect them or rejoin you in your endeavour to limn my likeness. They are of no little value, or import. Please guard them for me. Now, I must make haste to the country and wish you all success in your coming years.

Your friend
Elizabeth

I read the letter many times, finally reassembling it to its original state, as if I could reverse the import of its contents. I did not know quite why I was affected so much by this woman, older than me by perhaps five years, but she had imparted to me something of herself which I should do justice to, I felt. For now, I only had the solitary mannikin to help me honour that feeling, the spell she had over me, albeit I believed it was a benign spell.

Now, looking at her counterpart, I went over to it and brushed my fingers against the bodice, then down the skirt, wondering where their rightful wearer was right now. Was she indeed already gone?

I do not remember falling asleep, but I woke in the night to what I later learned to be the nightsoil men collecting in the street, going about their duty.

It came to me then, in the middle of the night, what I had to do. I had to recall her image and put it on the canvas. And *she* would aid me. *She* would be my guide. I would keep the clothes until I saw her again.

Before starting, I continued my letter to my father:

In the last days, a most unusual occurrence took place, and I write to you to ask your advice. A lady of noble birth, as I understand it, came to model for me for no stated reasons other than to assist Van Voerst, I presume, in pleasing me by giving me a useful and comely subject to work with for a portrait. As far as I know, no money was involved, but I have not asked. However, after my initial sketches and the action of transferring the sketches to the canvas, she did not return for another session. I took it upon myself to go to her house, but I received only a letter in return, with little explanation except a gift of the beautiful (and most valuable) clothes she had worn for her first sitting. Now, these clothes adorn the mannikin which you sent me and I will endeavour to do justice not only to the lady's beauty but also to the material and its lustre, which it emanates whenever the light is angled most propitiously. With your permission, I will keep and take care of these garments and bring them back to Holland when I return. Please say to Gesina that I am thinking of her always.

Your loving son
Gerard

Now, as I re-read this, I was suddenly overcome with impatience and decided I would put my thoughts down in a letter to the lady, regardless of whether she would ever see it. Just as I was about to proceed in this, I heard a knocking sound. At first I thought it might be someone in the street, someone drunk, or even the nightsoil men, but I realised it was the boy again. At this time! Two in the morning. It must be a most special event that would move him to try to wake me up now.

I opened the door, tentatively. He was standing there, with a lamp.

'Sir, I am sorry, but I have received a message that the lady is leaving soon. She wishes you to see her.'

The dress, I thought. She wants me to return it, perhaps.

'She said you need not bring anything except some paper and pens,' he said, meeting my thoughts before I could express them.

'Well,' I said. 'Take me back.'

'We will have to make the journey on foot, sir.'

'I understand. Let us go now.'

London at night. Whores in doorways. Dogs pissing at every vertical structure. Dead rats and cats in the kennels. I even thought I saw a dead, recently-born child in one. There were occasional shouts, even screams. Murderous? Not every house was lighted at this time, but as we reached the more salubrious area of town once more, there was the occasional lamp, and footmen stood in front of some doorways. This time, reaching the lady's house, we were allowed to enter by the front entrance on The Strand, to my relief.

What could she want now, at this time, exactly? I mulled as we were taken with no fuss through a large house, along a long corridor and up to what seemed a kind of gallery that had outside a walkway with a view of the Thames. On the way, I passed in the candlelight a series of paintings and sculptures the like of which I had never seen in one place. I saw pictures which I guessed to be the work of Tintoretto, Veronese, busts by all manner of sculptors, even engravings of works by Van Dyck. There were too many for me to be sure of their exact fashioners, but I ached to see them in the light. More than this, I ached to see *her* in the light.

Now, at the end of the corridor, she sat, showing only one side of her barely-lit face.

'Sir, you need not worry. No one is in the house, save a few servants, who will for once keep themselves to themselves.'

She winced as she said these last words.

'I have brought you here to ask you to finish your painting. I heard you have an intriguing mannikin?'

I looked at the boy, who was still with me. She nodded at him to leave.

'You have my clothes, you have seen my face in good light, albeit only once. Now, you will see it once more, and perhaps never again. And I will tell you my story until the light comes up and you can finish your work.'

I could not say anything. I would just listen.

'My father was . . . indiscreet with my . . . self, *and* my brother; he enlisted even the servants to his criminal bidding, at times. Do not worry, you will hear of these events publicly soon enough. I am only frightened that, should something happen to me, there would be little to show for it. I will in all likelihood survive. I am strong, but . . .'

She hesitated, for the first time.

'Perhaps I am vain, too. Perhaps I will yet find a suitor who will close his ears to everything he will doubtless hear and overcome the feeling to run from it. That would be truly noble.'

'A trial?' I offered.

'Indeed.'

Now, she described her childhood, a happy childhood, her loving mother and doting father. A childhood where nothing seemed awry. But when she was twelve years of age, she noticed a change in her father, of how he looked at her in a different way, of things he asked her to do without explanation. Of course, she could not argue. She could not show resistance.

The detail she permitted herself to delineate I will forego here. You, dear reader, will hear or will have heard all in the coming reports in all their clamorous outrage, I am certain. I will not re-enact for your pleasure what will doubtless incite further harm on this unfortunate woman.

As the light slowly came up, I found myself in two worlds, distracted by the opulence of the works around me, and the pulchritude of a face that I must do justice to and take back to my lonely room and work on till I could do no more, in the hope that one day she might see it. When I was finished and the servants started to move about this big empty house and I could see sail boats and lighters move up and down the river and hear the innocent cries of a new day, she walked me through the gallery, barely looking at the works on show. They were obviously the possessions of a monster; she could not endure to look on them any more, whereas I felt drunk by their mere beauty and sad that their possessor was a tyrant.

Once arrived back at my uncle's, I felt unable to explain anything to him as he stood there, expectantly. I did not feel able to communicate to anyone, however sympathetic they might be to my state of mind. I climbed the stairs like an old man, and, instead of going straight to my bed, I sat down in the chair that faced the window which was witness to the hubbub of the street below. I looked around the room for her and was startled to see she was not there, dress and all. Immediately, a surge of rage went through me, thinking she had been removed. I was about to run shouting downstairs demanding they tell me where she was, only, as I turned towards the door, my eye caught sight of an . . . elevation, of sorts, in my bed, under the cover. I moved slowly towards it, her, I thought; surely it was her. Now, almost in a fever, I raised the cover, and, yes, it was her, and she took me in her arms and I was enjoying pleasures to which I had never until that day been granted entry.

Epilogue

Dear Brother

I write in haste to make you aware of a most extraordinary situation that has arisen in my house and for which I am afraid I must take responsibility. Your son has, how shall I say, let himself become enamoured of a person to such an extent that, not foreseeing that something untoward might come of it, it has led him to retreat into himself, and more precisely, into his own room, so that for company he now has only that marvellous mannikin which you sent him. In itself I do not believe that it is such a terrible development – for he uses it constantly to paint a portrait – but that he speaks to it and to it alone. It is impossible to tear the poor fellow away from it, and I believe that on one occasion he used the word 'bride'. I am ashamed to be the bearer of such ill tidings, especially given that his talent is bounteous, to be sure, and improving all the time, but I implore you to come and fetch him, for his own good. I would furnish you with more background to the affair which I believe precipitated this situation, as far as I understand it, but that I can spare no more time before I send this post-haste. We will take the utmost care of him until your arrival. I enclose a letter which Gerard has been writing for some time and evidently could not bring to a satisfying end.

Yours loving brother, most urgently,
Robert

The Night Of São João

THE WORDS ARRIVED before their visual counterpart, a young woman of about twenty-two or -three, gliding in from the left, as he scanned the magical cityscape full of lanterns, small hot-air balloons which dotted the sky like the work of a modern artist who hadn't yet decided on the final pattern: 'It's not beautiful, Porto?' As little as he knew of the city, everything conspired to confirm her local origin: her accent was strong, with a deep timbre to it, and there was something slightly disconcerting about the syntax and intonation, as if she were continuing a conversation already started and had suddenly turned to him. Of course, she hadn't needed to check his nationality. She knew, or guessed, that he spoke English. The likelihood? Not huge, this evening of the Festival of São João, surely? But why him, now?

Only half an hour earlier, he had left his two female colleagues dancing in the road by the river Douro. He could not imagine finding them again tonight. It was pure chance that he had discovered this small triangular enclave containing a few trees, bordered on one side by the façade of a half-ruined, four-storeyed building, on another by a parapet that spread out its defining contour like the last hem of a large, many-pleated dress, and on a third by a church, though he predicted that, before long, this small bucolic niche would become uncomfortably crowded.

Extracts from his recent lecture still echoed in his mind. Had he got it right?

'... the double-slit experiment, where, according to the laws of quantum mechanics, an electron being aimed towards two vertical slits in a barrier emerges and hits the screen behind not as if it has definitely entered through one of the slits but rather somewhere on that screen that isn't necessarily in line with the path it has followed through the slit ...'

The young woman looked straight at him, her bow-lipped, open expression searching for something, some recognition. But he could be thirty years older than her, he thought. At least twenty, even if he was way off the mark.

This was the time to say something, if ever there was a time. Yet why would he think such a thing of a chance encounter with a stranger?

He had come at the suggestion of a colleague to give, and indeed had already delivered, a talk on a pet subject. In the few days he had left to himself, he was determined to take in as much as he could of the city without recourse to any online guide. A few leaflets from the hotel would suffice.

He looked after her, but she was already disappearing into a knot of people standing under a tree, as if she hadn't existed.

He persisted in looking into the dimness, with the fortuitous flare of light from another balloon that was just ascending, providing a temporary searchlight. No sign of her now.

Leaving that patch of ground, its throng, and the privileged view of the city, he walked slowly up an alley, then turned into a side street, where suddenly a woman put her hands around his waist. It wasn't her. This woman looked at him, fascinated for a few brief moments, said something in Portuguese he didn't understand, and, when he replied in English, she withdrew, looked disturbed, then laughed at something her companions had shouted out at her. He was relieved. She was plain and somewhat stunted in form, almost dwarf-like. Then he hated himself for thinking that way. Nevertheless, his last exchange with her as he looked back was an uncertain gavotte of timid smiles.

He turned another corner, realising he was back in the street he had exited to come out of the triangular patch in front of the parapet. So he was back in the same place! But he noticed a small family-run restaurant and decided to have a sangria.

He had to stand in line a while as mostly young people in their twenties came and went. It was not really unpleasant; it was just that the air was a little clammy.

A girl came in. She had a vaguely hippyish air, her back mostly bare, her particoloured, knitted top hinting at small breasts. He was aware that he was staring at her denimed backside, then at the soft part of flesh leading up to her armpit. Then he noticed she was with a much older man, probably her father, who stared back at him as they left. He didn't like the feeling and what was implied. He almost opened his mouth to explain himself. Too late.

He had had a vague intention to stay out till midnight, but deliberately held back from looking at his phone.

He had been living for years like this now, for just over a decade, living and teaching in different countries for three or four years at a time, since his divorce at the age of forty. The first marriage (both had been childless) had been a sincere attempt to make a success of truly falling in love with a stranger. Érzsi had been a third-year university student, he thirty, on the way to being a tenured professor, when they met, but they did not go out as a couple till after she had graduated. He had always loved the way she invariably put her long hair up in a small bundle, hiding its abundance, only unfurling it for special, private occasions. Her gold-rimmed glasses added an air of intellectuality at odds with her intuitive, sometimes impetuous nature, which early on had included an unrestrained interest in anyone and anything to do with Latin countries. She would stop and chat for ages with street musicians in ponchos on the streets of Budapest, often trying his patience. Eventually, they drifted apart, he leaving for England, she staying in Hungary, as far as he knew.

If his first marriage could have been described as tactical, then his second appeared to him now as strategic. As a partner, Emma was probably everything he would have avoided in earlier years: English, very self-controlled; a little prim, albeit with moments of abandon, from a higher social class than him, to be sure, but not a snob. She ran a small but respectable art gallery in London, and seemed very happy with her life, rubbing shoulders with moderately successful artists now and again. By the time she was thirty-eight, they had given up any pretensions of having a child, but, whilst they had tried, it was somehow understood that their attempts had been rather half-hearted. In the end, it could not truly have been claimed that they had any strong regrets at breaking up.

He realised he was caught up in a dense crowd, standing shoulder-to-shoulder with hundreds of others, at least that was how it felt. They were mainly much younger, lither, stronger than him. He had wandered into this predicament as if in a daydream from the cheery celebrating back streets on the hill, where there had been enough distance between people to avoid bumping into someone, although if you did, there was no palpable ill-feeling. But now in the Ribeira district, closer to the river, he was moving against a mass, part of a current headed, it seemed, to the river itself. When he had reached a point from which he could see no way of returning to his hotel along the river, he decided to work his way back up the hill in the hope that some spaces would open up as he ascended.

By a stroke of luck, he found himself in the train of a group of young men moving with ease through the dense crowd, so he positioned himself behind the last one. He was particularly large and muscular, managing to part the crowd with a winning charm that neutralised any potential friction – until they stopped in a square where everyone was standing still, he realised. The people all around were not exactly like statues, but for a brief moment he thought of moonlit scenes by Delvaux and the shadowed config-urations of de Chirico. Standing here like this, he felt a solitary body edge close to him. He did not want to turn round without good reason: the action of something or someone touching his hand was surely accidental. Then, the fireworks began.

He liked the things enough, but he was rarely stopped

in his tracks to view them, or would not have been if on this occasion he had not been held to the spot as he was. It was one pretty pattern after another, the eye anticipating and tracking geometric shapes and colours, the eyeball and neck alike straining to follow lines in the sky, to make sense of shapes that were there and then gone within seconds. Another bump, and a touch. It seemed like leather, warm for this weather, rubbing against his bare arm, doubtless impelled there by the tide of steadily moving, swaying bodies. Then he heard a self-conscious 'sorry', a slightly husky, familiar tone to it. As the colourful pyrotechnics above extended from a bearable fifteen minutes to a more trying thirty minutes, he was beginning to feel somewhat tired. At one point, he thought his legs might give way and he would have to hold on to someone or face being trampled on. Recovering just in time, he still felt her presence. She must be on her own.

Then, just as it seemed the display would carry on past the thirty-five-minute mark, it was over. The crowd expelled a mixture of regret and relief, shrunk in on itself, then spread out like a flower in a time-lapse film, mirroring the shapes it had so recently witnessed above it, then lost all sense of form as individuals and groups pushed their ways towards the nearest exit path.

And yet, amazingly, amongst all this, he felt a tug on his hand, this time more purposeful.

'Wait,' he heard.

He turned. It was the girl from earlier in the evening who had spoken to him about the view.

'Please, don't let go,' she went on, a slight tremolo in her voice.

'No, don't worry,' he said in an attempt to comfort her, but, laughing at himself and his predicament, he explained, unable to stop moving all the while, 'I don't really know where I'm going, to be honest . . . Are you lost?'

'Lost? No.'

'I mean, are you with someone you can't find?'

'Oh . . . no. It doesn't matter.'

'Are you sure?'

'Of course.'

They found a corner where they could stop a while without having to move while everyone filed up different alleys.

'Seems a shame,' he said, observing the scurrying shapes escaping from the square.

'What do you mean?'

'To just dissipate like that, so quickly.'

'Dissi . . . ?

'. . . pate. Like disappear.'

'Ah, dissipar.'

She paused a while, then looked up at him, giving, it seemed to him, an unearned amount of thought.

'How long are you in Porto?'

'Just two more days, unfortunately.'

'Oh! Can I show you some things?'

'What? Now?'

'Yes! The night is still young.'

'Well, I *am* free . . .'

She took his hand again.

They walked up the hill, and, seemingly aimlessly, downhill, then up again, passing several churches in the process. Although he wasn't religious, he could not help being disappointed at not being able to go in any of them.

'Don't worry, maybe tomorrow,' he heard her say.

'Are you reading my thoughts?' he nearly said, but held back. Just.

'I . . . I want to ask you, if you do not mind. Where do you come from?'

'Oh, England, originally. I spent a bit of time in a lot of countries, France, Germany, Hungary.'

'Hungary?'

'Have you been?'

'No, never, just . . .'

She trailed off.

'You're a student, right?'

'And you're a teacher?'

'Ah, touché. You can see that so easily?'

'I . . . didn't mean to say you were old . . .'

'No, no, I wasn't thinking that.'

She looked at him directly, coming slightly closer, leaning in, to a point that made him self-conscious.

Those almond eyes. Their darkness. Their depth. It was not the typical look he went for.

'So, you are in Porto for what?'

'I just did a talk, a lecture. It's a bit of a mishmash. About energy, sustainability, security, the state of the nuclear arsenals. You know, nuclear weapons.'

'New . . . ?'

'Armas nucleares? I think you say.'

'Really? Tell me about them.'

He felt a sense of dread coming on. Not at the subject matter itself, but at his propensity to talk shop, to put people off with jargon, to stun people with statistics, especially students, to point out how many multiple warheads were on just one of the many American, British, Russian, or French submarines. But his captive audience's abilities to comprehend such pointed details often soon waned, leaving them incapable of seeing the bigger picture, as if they were trying to count the stars in a galaxy.

'In short, there are too many, way too many.'

'One is too many, surely.'

Now *he* was stunned. Perceptive. In an age where the Cold War had been almost forgotten, till very recently, and people around the world were focused on the minutiae of their daily, mostly online lives, seemingly only interested in seeing themselves reflected, their every second of life an instantly publishable event.

'And what about you? What are you studying?'

'Film history. It's fascinating.'

'I'm sure. It's always been an interest of mine.'

She pulled her hair up suddenly, bunching it. A memory stirred.

'I feel sticky.'

'Maybe it's the sulphur in the air from all those explosions.'

Her reaction was a 'Huh' and a wry look. 'Shall we go down to the river? There are so many places to drink, even eat, if you want,' she enthused.

'Sure, let's go, then.'

'Tell me more about nu . . . clear weapons,' she said, once they were seated in a bar on the river front.

He did a double take. It was a first, this, whether from a swotty student or an acquaintance who was just being polite.

'I can't . . .'

He wanted to say he couldn't explain *everything*, of course, but that was lame; in this case, he was being invited to do exactly that.

He thought of a friend who liked to take photos of sunrises with distorted colours so that they looked like nuclear explosions.

'You have to start from the present, think about how many weapons there are in the world right now, and who has them. Care to take a guess?'

'You mean how many?'

'Yes.'

'I don't know. Five hundred?'

'Somewhat more.'

'I know North Korea has some, maybe two or three.'

'It's about 14,000. The US and Russia have the majority, about 6,000 each.'

There was a silence he could only describe as shocked. Then, like a delayed impact, came her words:

'Oh my God, oh my God, oh my God. Oh . . . my . . . God.'

He could not resist feeling a strange sense of satisfaction at her reaction.

'I thought . . .'

'They were all gone?'

'Almost . . . yes.'

While her mouth was still agape, he started in on how this number had been greatly reduced since the heyday of the arms race, which took him back to various emergencies and preparations for nuclear war, the SIOP system, a first strike by the US which would have taken care of not only the Soviet Union but also China, for good measure.

'Well, anyway, there's a long way to go before we get to zero nukes,' he concluded. 'Only the race is just starting up all over again.' He could have gone on, about the danger of weapons not being maintained properly, about the new American nuclear 'posture', Putin's new hypersonic nuclear weapons, the 'low-yield', tactical weapons, but it was not that he was an expert in weapons per se.

'Wow.'

'Yes, wow.' Then, 'You've surely heard enough of this now.'

Seeing it was already one-thirty, he didn't want to go back.

'Tell me about Porto, please.'

'I want to *show* you Porto, but we need the light, I think. It would be so nice to see the sunrise.'

'Essential, even.'

'Yes, essential. I like that.'

'We need to pass some time in a wine cellar. On the other side of the river? It's just too noisy here, anyway.'

'Yes, I know where we can go.'

They made their way along the Douro, against the dregs of the crowd, which moved in a Day-Glo haze of bare arms, legs, hot pants, illuminated plastic hammers, and streamers, like something out of a film by Gaspar Noé. He felt only slightly conscious of his age as they walked together, but no one seemed to care. No funny looks at the pair of them. They both got hit over the head with the hammers on a number of occasions; when he asked her about it, she explained it was a modern variation on a very old courtship ritual.

On the way, there was plenty to comment on: the shell of an old building high up from the road, perhaps once a patrician's town house or even a small factory, with open, impractical doorways and an impossible arch he felt like walking through; a closed baroque church covered in blue-and-white tiles; a sequence of four-and-five-storeyed terraced houses with balconies and tiles in various geometric combinations, sometimes containing Maltese crosses, sometimes rhombuses, sometimes dizzying floral patterns.

They reached and crossed the busy lower deck of the narrow iron Luis I bridge, walking single file, she pulling on his hand a few times to steady herself so that she didn't fall into the road from the raised pavement as motorbikes and taxis sped by. The other side, the Gaia, starting with the Avenue de Diogo Leite, seemed to cater for more sophisticated tastes, chief of which was wine.

It was hard to find a place that wasn't full, but she had an idea. As they turned a corner, he was for a moment stopped in his tracks. Standing sentry on the corner of another street a little way up, a giant rabbit four or five metres high was staring him down, its eyes unblinking. The animal seemed to emanate from the building itself, to be an outgrowth of it. One side of it was varicoloured. The whiskers looked particularly menacing.

'What . . . ?'

She seemed to be stifling her amusement as she noticed his reaction. It took a few paces, but he soon realised: it was just a sculpture made of various pieces of junk, metal, wood, crushed plastic containers, and many artfully placed feathers. Basically, it was one huge Rauschenberg *combine*.

As she finally burst out laughing, he made a feint like a boxer punching her on the arm; they came together, awkwardly, holding each other in a semi-embrace. What must he seem like to her, he wondered, conscious of his browning teeth, his sagging skin. Two options played themselves out in his mind. If she saw him as a father figure, she might not ponder these aspects of his physical decay, but if she saw him as a potential lover, crazy as that seemed to him, she was likely to be repulsed, even if she had only entertained the thought fleetingly.

Yet, they were still holding on to each other and he became aware of a solidity to her small limbs, guessing she was agile but strong; he felt the hard presence of her brassiere.

They went into a timbered hall, which had plenty of wooden tables and some upturned barrels. There was even enough space to move around, surprisingly.

'It's your turn to tell me about Porto now.'

'It's not light enough yet.'

'I'd like to see some churches.'

'You are Católico?'

'No, no. I'm not really . . .'

'Don't worry. I was just born Cath . . . lic?'

He nodded.

'I mean there are so many beautiful churches. I've only glimpsed . . .'

'Let's see. Where have you been so far?'

They were on their second glass of port now. He tried to describe a number of places he'd seen, but his descriptions were vague, and she looked confused for perhaps the first time since they had met.

Then, she almost shouted out: 'Oh, I know! Have you taken photos, with your phone?'

'Yes.'

'We can locate any places you've been exactly, you know.'

'Oh, really?'

He sort of knew what she meant, but he generally resisted availing himself of all those digital bells and whistles.

'I don't really use it that much . . .'

'Can I see?'

'What?'

'Your photos. If you don't have secrets, that is.'

'Oh, of course not.'

'Oh.' She looked suddenly downbeat.

'I mean, of course you can. I don't have any secrets!'

He took out his phone and started scrolling back to when he had arrived. She pulled her stool around to him so they could look together, leaning into him in the process.

'You see, here, this church, São Pedro de Miragaia.'

It was the one he remembered by the river being completely covered in the blue tiles.

'Scroll up to the map below, then click on the photo on the map, then "information", then "hybrid", then "3D". That's right. You twist it around with your fingers, so . . . you can see all sides of a building, from every angle, like in real life, and it's showing other photos you've taken, too, if you zoom out again.'

'Excellent,' he said. 'I hadn't quite realised you could do all *that*. I've barely got the hang of swiping yet,' he added half-jokingly.

'I can't believe that, *professor*,' she teased him. 'What else did you see?'

He hovered his finger over the photos he had taken in the area.

Not sure exactly why, he tapped on another church where he remembered standing near a square.

'Now,' she said. 'This is Sé do Porto, the cathedral.'

He resisted the urge to say he could see that, on the map.

Confidently, she moved the 3D image around so that they were looking at a small terrace of buildings that looked very familiar to him. Some were four storeys high, some five, and definitely not completely perpendicular, leaning this way and that. Then he saw he had taken his own photos of this area, of these very buildings. There they were, in reasonable proximity to the graphic for him to just about be able to confirm the fact.

'Those are the same buildings as on the 3D map, aren't they?'

'Yes, I think you're right,' she said, a slight smile seeming to edge its way over her face. But he was concentrating on the images and the map: he must have taken these from the steps leading down from the cathedral, in the shadow of its twin towers.

Here, in more detail, in his own photo, he could make out buttresses holding up the end building on the right, two brown front doors giving straight onto the street, then, above, on the first, second, and third floors, the ubiquitous tiles, as well as various blue-and-yellow streamers attached to the second-floor balcony ready for the celebrations to come and that had now passed. Next to the house with the brown doors was another four-storey building with two green front doors, its façade barer, with no tiles, a rickety-looking shuttered first floor, a quaint bay of white-latticed windows on the third, and finally, on the fourth, another layer of shutters, this time with a football cup design on the left-hand shutter. Going further to the left, there was another four-storey, but it was taller, and next to that one, a five-storey house, making one realise that its shorter companions were in some way compressed, by comparison.

'Very picturesque! It's the mediaeval part, you know? We'll go there, when it's light,' she said.

'For sure,' he agreed.

They drank and talked till about six in the morning. He had a vague memory of talking about the double-slit experiment: *'in other words,'* he half-recalled, *'there's a possibility the electron has entered through one of the slits, except it can't be said for sure by which slit it has entered. Ultimately, this is because the electron is behaving as a wave, called a probability wave, spreading out as it goes through one of the slits.'*

They left, supporting each other through the winding streets. There were very few clues to the previous evening's revels now, the streamers and flattened, singed carcases of balloons apart. Gulls stood around or stepped circumspectly, as if sensitive to people's inevitable hangovers.

They found themselves staggering down Calçada das Virtudes, which on one side was lined with a rather magnificent ashlared wall with arched recesses, towards the Jardim Municipal do Horto das Virtudes. At the bottom of the incline, they found themselves facing a wall, into which was set a baroque design of pilasters and a coat of arms.

'It's the Fonte das Virtudes, the Fountain of Virtues,' she said, suddenly alert, almost as if she were seeing it for the first time.

'Doesn't look like much of a fountain,' he replied, sounding more nonchalant than he had intended.

She ribbed him gently, smiling.

'It's old,' was her sole response.

They continued down through the winding streets, passing at one point through a tunnel of corrugated iron and scaffolding over one alley, till they came out to the river, where they found a place to have breakfast.

'We should see the cathedral, don't you think?' she suggested.

They decided to climb once more up the hill into the mediaeval part where they had been during the festival, to see it in daylight, properly. He was still amazed at how she had so much time for him, a stranger.

On the way, he went into various shops selling touristy knick-knacks, the most common of which were small tiles and mugs with blue-and-white Moorish designs. She seemed to look around with equal interest, he thought, though she was supposed to be from this city.

Just as they reached each other, their eyes fell simultaneously on some postcards.

'Oh, look,' she pointed out, 'isn't that where you took a photo?'

'Yes. The old houses.'

'Near the cathedral.'

That does it, he thought.

He bought two of the same postcard, giving one to her, and took her hand, surprising himself at his boldness.

It wasn't long before they were at the cathedral. They walked around the many parts of the building, which had a cloister and enfilades of hallways. At one point, he lost her, and walked around, slightly despairing, trying to conjure up her image in his mind, should he never see her again. Then, she walked through one of the many doorways, back into his life, oblivious of his worry, as if from another dimension.

'I . . . thought I'd lost you.'

'Silly!' she said, taking his hand. 'Now, let's see that view!'

They came out the front, with the twin towers casting a shadow over them. She pulled him, with more sense of purpose than before, to the right, exactly where the parapet faced the old houses.

'You have the photo you took?'

'Yes, and the card.'

They started to compare the photo on his phone with that on the card and with the buildings in front of them.

'It's amazing,' she said.

'What?'

'There are so many differences.'

'Like what?'

'Well, no washing hangs out now, or in your photo, like on the card,' she said, referring to the house with the green doors. She was studying the card intensively, barely looking at the buildings themselves.

'And the shutters are down on the fourth floor, but not on the card,' he contributed.

'Hmm. And there's a white plaque over the second green door of the house on the left, on the card,' she added.

'The streamers are new, of course,' he said referring to the present, and added, 'but the blue-and-white tiles on the house on the right with the brown doors are still there, of course.'

'And yet,' he went on, 'the third-floor windows look different, as if they've been completely changed.'

Then, shifting back to the house on the left with the green doors: 'The sheet of corrugated iron on the third floor here, with the balcony. That's been added. As if they wanted to be cut off from communicating with the people on the balcony of the taller building next door.'

'Corru . . . ?'

'The sheet of iron, rippled, like waves.'

'Ah, *ferro corrugado*, yes. Or maybe it's just to protect from the sun?'

'Could be,' he conceded.

He went on, 'So why are there two entrances, side-by-side?'

He stopped for a moment. He was having a déjà vu episode, for maybe the first time since his childhood.

As more electrons pass through the slits, a pattern can be found on the screen that shows the different places electrons from the same beam have hit it.

He remembered now, telling her.

And yet, if a detector is placed at the slits, then it behaves as a particle that definitely only entered through one specific slit.

'It reminds me of the double-slit experiment I was telling you about.'

'A bit like you and me?'

'How do you mean?'

'Well, we are together, now. You must choose one of the entrances, but you have no idea, without a sign.'

He put his arm around her shoulder; she rested her head in the crook of his neck.

'Are you that sign? Or am I going crazy?' he pursued.

She stayed silent. Something caught her attention. A middle-aged woman appeared on the balcony of the green house, directly above one of the doors. She was waving. His companion noticed her and made a gesture that might have been acknowledgement of the older woman's wave. As if deliberately, almost like a movie star, this older woman reached behind her, loosened the hidden bun of hair, and shook it down.

'I think it's time to find out,' she said.

Acknowledgements

The Shore – originally published in *Infra Noir,* Issue No.1,
summer, 2018

Green To Blue – originally published in *The Third
Alternative*, issue 23

The Mask – originally published in *Milk: An Anthology of
Eroticism*, edited by Sophie Essex, *2017,* reprinted in *Best
British Short Stories 2018*, ed. Nicholas Royle

The Transfer – originally published in *Night Train* 8.1
(online and POD), 2008.

Meeting Julie Christie – originally published in *Time Out
Net Books*, Vol.4, online, 1995, edited by Nicholas Royle

The Night of São João – to be published in *Cōnfingō* (anthology), spring 2022.

I would like to thank the following friends for all their
suggestions, help, and support over the years and the various
iterations of these stories: Mark Alberding (portrait photo-
graph), Ken Anderson, Jo Barris, Kate Brown, Benson
Cabuelo, Gary Couzens, Judith Dancoff, Sophie Essex,
Daniel Ferreira, Dave Gann, Susan Hodges, Andrew Hook,
Alison Kettering, José Luis, Martin Kemp, Jai King-Clare,

Saskia van der Linden, Ellen Motohashi, Jonas Ploeger, Nicholas Royle, Matthew Ryan, Leo Stevenson, Wendy Vaizey, Cecilia Ai Villacis, James Wilcox, Evan Williams.

This book has been typeset by
SALT PUBLISHING LIMITED
using Granjon, a font designed by George W. Jones
for the British branch of the Linotype company in the
United Kingdom. It is manufactured using Holmen
Book Cream 70gsm, a Forest Stewardship Council™
certified paper from the Hallsta Paper Mill in Sweden.
It was printed and bound by Clays Limited in Bungay,
Suffolk, Great Britain.

CROMER
GREAT BRITAIN
MMXXII